"I suppose that's all okay." Sara looked from Bunkhouse 13 to the chuck wagon. "At least if he needs me, I'm not far away."

"I'm sure you don't want Mickey treated any different than the other seven wranglers whose mothers aren't here. Right?"

"But I *am* here, Mr. Beaumont."

"Mrs. Peterson, please, give him some room."

She rolled her eyes. "Is that your professional advice?"

"Nope. It's my gut feeling," Jesse said.

"What else does your gut tell you?" she asked.

"That you have to relax, and I'm just the cowboy to show you how."

Dear Reader,

Welcome back to Beaumont, Oklahoma, the home of the three bull-riding Beaumont brothers: Luke, Reed and Jesse. They are all Gold Buckle Cowboys.

This is Jesse Beaumont's story.

Jesse would rather be doing anything but wrangling a bunch of kids at Camp Care, but he soon grows to like them all, especially Sara Peterson's son, Mickey, who hasn't spoken a word since his father died in a car accident. Unfortunately, Mickey was in the same accident.

Jesse and Sara don't agree on anything, least of all how to deal with Mickey. After all, Jesse is the boy's ramrod, but Sara is the boy's mother. Jesse doesn't have any credentials other than that he can ride bulls, but the kids of Camp Care—along with the entire female staff!—seem to be caught up in Jesse's charisma.

Life is good here in central New York. As I write this, there is a foot of snow on the ground and the Professional Bull Riders (PBR) are going to be at Madison Square Garden starting their next season of competition.

Yee haw!

Christine Wenger

HOME *on the* RANCH

OKLAHOMA BULL RIDER

— ⚒ —

CHRISTINE WENGER

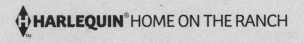

Recycling programs
for this product may
not exist in your area.

ISBN-13: 978-1-335-00560-1
ISBN-13: 978-1-335-63395-8 (Direct to Consumer edition)

Home on the Ranch: Oklahoma Bull Rider

Printed in U.S.A.

www.Harlequin.com

Christine Wenger has worked in the criminal-justice field for more years than she cares to remember, but now spends her time reading, writing and seeing the sights in our beautiful world. A native central New Yorker, she loves watching professional bull riding and rodeo with her favorite cowboy, her husband, Jim. You can reach Chris at PO Box 1823, Cicero, NY 13039, or through her website at christinewenger.com.

Books by Christine Wenger

Harlequin Western Romance

Gold Buckle Cowboys

The Cowboy and the Cop
Reunited with the Bull Rider

Harlequin Special Edition

Gold Buckle Cowboys

The Rancher's Surprise Son
Lassoed into Marriage
How to Lasso a Cowboy
The Cowboy Code

The Hawkins Legacy

The Tycoon's Perfect Match
It's That Time of Year

Not Your Average Cowboy
The Cowboy and the CEO
The Cowboy Way

Visit the Author Profile page
at Harlequin.com for more titles.

To my dear brother, John Matyjasik, who is strong, silent and has a heart of gold. I love you.

And to the memories of Ed Francis, Eddie Francis and Joan Paries. Rest in peace.

Chapter 1

"Jesse Daniel Beaumont, will you stand and approach the bench, please?"

Jesse did as instructed.

Justice Richard Connor leaned over his huge oak desk, looked down upon him from a high platform and whispered, "Jess, a bar fight?" He sighed. "I remember those days. Your brother Luke and I got into some doozies."

"Ricky, technically, it wasn't a bar fight. It was outside the bar in the parking lot."

"You bull riders and bronc riders have to stop fighting, for heaven's sake." The judge kicked up the volume of his voice, probably for the benefit of the spectators in the courtroom.

Judge Connor couldn't show favoritism to one of

the town of Beaumont's leading citizens and one of his oldest friends.

Ricky continued, "Mr. Beaumont, this matter is a violation of the law, not a felony or misdemeanor. A lawyer is not necessary in this court, but this matter will be adjourned should you wish to obtain one."

"No, thanks, Your Honor. Let's just get this over with. The bronc riders decided to blow off some steam, and—"

The judge raised a thick black eyebrow and whispered, "I don't care who started it, but I have to hold you to a higher standard since Beaumont—"

Jesse nodded. "Was founded by my ancestor." Jesse had heard it all before, many times. "And you need to make an example out of me. Right, Ricky?"

"Sheesh. Keep your voice down, Jess." The judge looked stern, but still whispered. "Camp Care over in Conifer Hill needs some wranglers to live and work with the horses and the kids. You'd be perfect."

"What are you saying?" Jesse shook his head. "You want me to wrangle kids?"

"No, I don't want you to wrangle kids! Shut up, Jess, and let me finish. In July, Camp Care opens for boys with special needs. You know, equine therapy. Riding horses strengthens their bones, gives them confidence, responsibility and a great role model in the form of a bunkhouse ramrod for a month. Well, maybe you're not a great role model right now, but you're a natural with kids. They love you."

"They like me because I'm a sports figure, but aww…c'mon, Ricky. A whole month? I have things to do at the ranch while I'm on summer break from the Professional Bull Riders. You know, the Beaumont Ranch is still rebuilding after Hurricane Chloe and my brothers are building houses, and I'd like to help them.

"Can't you just let me go?"

"Sure. If you promise me that you'll work at Camp Care and that you'll stay away from bronc riders." Okay, one more try to convince Ricky that he wasn't the right cowboy for the job.

"Speaking of bronc riders, after they were arrested, all you gave them was a fine."

"I know, but you're a great horseman, and Camp Care needs you."

"But those bronc riders practically live on horses! They would have been perfect for Camp Care."

"Nope. You're the one. You'd be a terrific bunkhouse ramrod and horse wrangler," Ricky said quickly. "C'mon, Jess, will you do it? Camp Care needs the help."

"Bunkhouse ramrod? Does that mean what I think it does, Ricky?"

"Eight kids to a bunkhouse with basically the same needs and one bunkhouse ramrod. That'll be you. You'll be given extra training by the best psychologists, school and medical personnel. And they will always be available to assist you."

"I know that Camp Care is a special charity of yours, and I've been promising to help you out for a couple of years now." Jesse took a deep breath. "I'll be glad to help out during July."

There went his plans to help his brothers build their houses.

"Yeah. Okay. And I'll assist the kids when they ride horses, too."

Maybe he was sweating for nothing.

Jesse regularly helped out whenever the Professional Bull Riders sponsored equine programs for the kids before an event in various states, and he took a training class on the side. He figured he could handle whatever Camp Care needed him to do while standing on his head.

Yeah, right. Who was he kidding?

But Jesse was trapped and he knew it. He didn't mind helping the kids ride, but living with a bunkhouse full of them for a whole month? That would try the best counselors, and he wasn't a counselor by a long stretch. In fact, he was more nervous about living with the kids and counseling them than he was straddling a two-thousand-pound bull with baseball bats for horns. He needed to help his family build their houses. The Beaumont brothers had always stuck together, since their days of playing musketeers.

The judge nodded. "Oh, and would you mind autographing one of your riding gloves for Stevie? You're his favorite of the Beaumont Big Guns. His birthday is coming up, and he'd be higher than a kite if he got one of your signed gloves."

"Sure." Jesse grinned. "I think I have a riding glove in the car or in my gear bag at home. I'll get it to you."

The judge motioned for him to go back to his seat, then spoke in a booming voice. "Mr. Beaumont, please return to your seat and face the bench."

"Mr. Jesse Daniel Beaumont, how do you plead, guilty or not guilty?"

Jesse ground his teeth. Okay, he did throw a couple of punches, but he'd tried to break up a couple fights, too.

"Guilty, Your Honor."

"Jesse Beaumont, you are hereby sentenced to a conditional discharge with the condition that you complete a month of community service at Camp Care on a full-time basis during the month of July. When your community service is satisfactorily completed, your charge will be dismissed. I will appoint an individual at Camp Care to report back to the court as to your progress, or lack thereof. If you fail to complete your community service, the charge against you will be reinstated and you'll be sentenced to a period of time at the Beaumont County Jail."

Jail time at the same institution that proclaimed his family's name in blazing metal letters over the entrance? The same institution that his father spent some time in? If he was incarcerated there, too, the walls would come crumbling down!

"Thank you, Your Honor," Jesse said respectfully. "I will do my best." He felt like he was participating in a play, but only he and Ricky were in on the secret.

"See that you do, Mr. Beaumont." He tapped his index finger on his bench. "And no more fighting, please."

"Yes, Your Honor."

As Jesse walked out of the courtroom and down the steps, he convinced himself that he didn't have to worry about his community service at all. It wasn't as if he were a rookie; he'd had some practice with the PBR, and he had a whole Camp Care staff to help him.

He knew about horses, and damn, he sure knew about bulls, and he knew how to handle just about every other livestock animal on the planet. His mom had been famous for bringing injured animals home and letting her three boys nurse them back to health.

With kids, he was a rookie; with horses and bulls, not so much.

Whenever he thought about his mother, he remembered how he lost her when he was sixteen. It seemed like only yesterday that she'd been kicked by a horse and had died in his father's arms on the way to the hospital. Big Dan Beaumont hadn't been the same since.

But after long years on probation, a diligent probation officer, and months in alcohol rehab, at least Big Dan was sober now instead of being the town menace.

Someday, he'd like to find the love that his parents had. So far, he was busy dodging buckle bunnies and making sure they didn't sneak into his hotel room when he was on the road or corner him at one of his autograph events.

As Jesse got into his big black pickup truck that he'd received as a gift from one of his corporate sponsors, he chuckled. Big Dan and he had both been accused of fighting, only the difference was that Jesse hadn't been drinking, and he hadn't wrecked a couple of bars like his father.

Jesse had been coming out of a charity event at the fairgrounds, he and a bunch of other riders. He didn't know who said what or who threw the first punch, but they'd all scattered like the wind when the cops came. He hadn't moved, because the thought of running from his sister-in-law, Beaumont County Sheriff Amber Chapman Beaumont, seemed ludicrous.

But it wasn't Amber who was on patrol that evening. On duty were two deputies and two rookies who were so fast they must have won gold medals for track and field in the Olympics.

When Sergeant Jay Prestin whizzed by, he said, "Jesse, stay put. Don't move a muscle."

So he stayed put and didn't move a muscle.

"Jay, cut me some slack, will you?"

"Aww, Jess. I wish I could, but I arrested six bronc riders and couldn't very well let you go."

While handing him an appearance ticket, Jay apologized to him. "Sorry, Jess. Normally, I wouldn't have even made any arrests for disorderly conduct, but one of the bar patrons had complained that two combatants had landed on his opened-top convertible and were brawling on his front seat, then flipped to his back seat, and vice versa and crushed some of his opera CDs like potato chips."

"That wasn't me, Jay. I did my fighting in the parking lot."

Jesse shook his head at the memory and turned left onto the "highway," Trish Perkins Road, which was posted at fifty miles an hour. That was a lot of speed for Beaumont with Trish's twists and turns.

He turned right onto—*what else?*—Beaumont Road, which led to the ranch. He drove under the wrought iron arch that said—*what else?*—Beaumont Ranch with *B*'s and some tasteful scrollwork.

Whenever he drove under the arch, he thought about the unbelievable history that he'd inherited. With that history came responsibility. He and his brothers did what they could to help fellow ranchers and neighbors get good prices for their stock, and when their neighbors found themselves in financial trouble, a windfall suddenly appeared.

Sure, the homestead was founded when Ezra Beaumont was alleged to have jumped the gun a little too soon and first claimed this parcel, but throughout the years, his ancestors had added land, horses and cattle to the ranch, and established the town.

A sense of responsibility to his heritage had been instilled into him on a regular basis. He always felt the pressure to live up to Beaumont family standards. That was why it had hurt him to see his father become the local drunk and the town joke. But many of their good neighbors and friends knew that Big Dan had been mourning his wife with liquor and bar fights.

To this day, the schoolchildren of Beaumont had

to learn the history. They also received tours of the grounds and the historic ranch house every two years along with a barbecue and a singalong with the Cowhand Band.

When he wasn't on the road riding bulls, Jesse enjoyed being home. Right now, both of his older brothers were building houses on their land, and Jesse planned on helping out. He loved construction work, but now in a couple of weeks, he had to be heading for Camp Care. It was at the upper left corner of Beaumont County, and he could commute back and forth, but he had a sinking feeling that he'd be staying at the camp around the clock unless he could talk his "handler" into letting him go home.

It all depended on how he took to his job of a bunkhouse ramrod and horse wrangler.

Sara Peterson drove the gray rental car onto the rutted Camp Care driveway. Her budget only allowed her to keep it for a week, but she was sure that she'd know if this place was going to help Mickey by then.

If the answer was "no," she'd ask for a refund and the two of them would fly back immediately.

The instruction booklet, which she'd almost memorized, indicated that she should check in at the administrative office. There it was, on her left. In keeping with the cowboy theme, a sign said "Assay Office. Miners Welcome. File your claim here."

She pitied those who hadn't read the booklet carefully. They'd be looking for a sign that said Admin-

istrative Office instead of an old miner's shack...
ahem...assay office.

She had to look up "assay." Basically, it was an office set up to examine rocks for gold, silver or copper
and to file claims on property. These valuable met-
als were what the miners strove for in an attempt to
hit it big. Some did, most didn't. Sara looked around
at all the rustic buildings that seemed as if they all
could use new paint and even newer roofs. Was this
derelict mess what she'd scrimped and saved for?
The place that she'd lost her job over because Charles
Ryan and Son Appliances wouldn't give her a leave
of absence? Was this the place that was supposed to
help her ten-year-old son speak again?

She saw some kids in wheelchairs and recumbent
bikes. Some had guide dogs and walked in pairs of
two or three or more. She hoped that Mickey would
find friends here.

Her once talkative and joyful Mickey, now silent
and so alone for more than two years.

She loved to run her fingers through his black hair,
so soft and shiny. His big brown eyes, once twin-
kling, were now dimmed with sadness and melan-
choly. Mickey, who used to do wheelies on his bicycle
and raced his bike with his friends, now sat silent and
isolated. His spindly legs and knobby knees, which
once propelled him to make basket after basket, now
were under his desk while he played on his computer.

Sara pulled into a parking space, shut her car off
and looked at Mickey. He was staring straight ahead
at the assay office.

"Mickey, let's get you registered and then you'll get a cabin. Isn't this going to be fun?"

No answer.

It wasn't as *if* Sara had expected one, but she could always hope.

If this ramshackle place could get her son to talk, then losing her job and working off some of Mickey's tuition in the camp kitchen would be worth it.

"Okay, Mickey. Let's go check in."

As she walked up the stairs, which were surprisingly sturdy for the old building, she silently cursed Charles Ryan and Son. Since old Charlie Ryan retired and his son took over Charles Ryan and Son Appliances, Ryan Junior wouldn't hear of her taking leave in the summer. He said that was their busiest time. Even when she explained about Mickey and how she was going to work in Camp Care's kitchen in exchange for having some of her son's camp tuition waived, Charlie Junior stood firm.

How much business could an appliance place have during the summer in little Henderson Falls, New York? That was when most took their vacations.

She'd worked there since she was eighteen, designing spreadsheets, entering all kinds of appliance information, ordering stock and parts and putting in orders for repairs. In all of those ten years, she'd never noticed a spike in appliance sales in the summer. In fact, business declined.

Then Junior had let her go, saying that his wife was going to take over Sara's job anyway to save him money.

She was outraged and stormed out of the place, but not before dumping her "things to do" basket all over Junior's desk. Then she combed the classified ads and went out for numerous job interviews. Nothing had come through. When she'd called Lori Floyd, the business manager of Camp Care, and told her that her insurance had been terminated and that their round-trip airline tickets from Syracuse to Beaumont, Oklahoma, took up the last of her savings, the wonderful woman told her that the cost of Mickey's stay would be covered, and would she like to work in the kitchen?

Absolutely!

Maybe, Charlie Ryan Junior would figure out that he couldn't get along without her and ask her back.

But she wouldn't go back to Charles Ryan and Son Appliances. She'd take great pleasure in turning Junior down. Especially when she'd been treated miserably and left crying and wondering how she'd get the money for all of Mickey's counselors. Where would she get the money for their next round of groceries when they returned to New York? Unemployment and food stamps were a blessing, but they didn't cover everything she needed.

She wasn't going to ask her parents for money anymore. As it was, they were paying for a lot of Mickey's psychiatrist fees. They were on a fixed income. She wouldn't ask them for one more cent.

Sara's meager savings paid for his other counselors and whatever else he needed, like specialized doctors who all said that there was nothing physical wrong with Mickey's ear canals or his throat nor any other sign of trauma from the accident.

So the diagnosis was PTSD and selective mutism from the accident.

The last psychiatrist that she'd taken him to endorsed Camp Care very highly. So, clinging to her recommendation, she started the wheels turning... or should she say *wagon* wheels?

Sara had to think positive. Maybe being let go was a sign that it was time for a change. Charles Ryan and Son Appliances was a dead end anyway.

They walked into the Assay Office, where the theme continued. Yellowed "Wanted" posters littered the gray, wooden walls. There were signs detailing the prices for a bath. She had to smile at the descriptions. A tub of water and a sliver of soap, could be had for fifty cents. A clean towel was an extra twenty-five cents.

"Hello and welcome to Camp Care! I'm Lori Floyd, Camp Care's administrator. Who is this young man? Is he going to be one of our wranglers?"

Mickey stared straight ahead oblivious of Lori Floyd's cheerful demeanor.

"I'm Sara Peterson, and this is my son, Mickey."

"Hi, Sara! And welcome, Mickey. Let me check you in. I love checking in our wranglers."

Mickey was seemingly oblivious to her excitement. Tears stung Sara's eyes when she remembered how Mickey used to play any game that involved a ball or stick. Now, he just sat and watched TV. Even with the crazy comedies on, Mickey never cracked a smile.

"Just call me Lori. We're pretty informal here at the Double C."

"Okay. Lori it is. And please, call me Sara. We spoke on the phone. And I'd like to thank you for everything you've done. I'm sure that Mickey's thrilled to be here."

Lori waved the air dismissing her gratitude. "No problem." She picked up a sheet of paper. "And you're going to work in our chuck wagon, right, Sara? You'll have a great time with everyone, especially Phil. He's the chef, also known as Cookie. I'll check Mickey in, then Mickey can go to his bunkhouse for a bag lunch. We do that on moving-in day. After you drop Mickey off, go to the chuck wagon and have some lunch, and you can let Phil know you're here and pick up your schedule. You'll be serving dinner tonight. Did you bring your cowgirl duds to wear?"

"Yes. I brought jeans and boots and a couple of long-sleeved blouses," Sara replied.

"Perfect." Lori turned her attention to Mickey. "Mickey, a chuck wagon is what accompanied the trail drives in the old days. Usually, the cook drove the wagon and all his supplies were there—pots and pans, flour, coffee, bacon, tin plates and cups. That's why we call our food hall the chuck wagon."

There wasn't any visible interest from Mickey.

Lori kept talking. "And, Mickey, we have a wonderful cabin for you with a wonderful ramrod. That means he's the boss of the bunkhouse, just like a ramrod was the cowboy in charge of the cattle and the cowboys in the old days. Everyone had to listen to him. Your ramrod is a little new, but you can break him in." She giggled.

"He's a local guy," Lori said, typing on a laptop. "Oh, and, Mickey, he's a top bull rider with the Professional Bull Riders. You are going to like him a lot. He's definitely cool." Lori had a dreamy expression on her face.

"Sara, you are in Bunkhouse 16. Mickey, you are in Bunkhouse 13." Lori scribbled on a yellow piece of paper. "And, Mickey, your ramrod is Jesse Beaumont. He is volunteering to serve out a sentence of community service. The town and county of Beaumont was even named for his ancestor, who founded the town. And you two flew into the Beaumont Airport, I'm sure."

"Jesse Beaumont," Sara repeated. She was betting her last cent on the skills of this…um…bull rider to help her son?

A bull rider?

"Oh," Lori puffed up her hair, and hurriedly slid on a bright slash of lipstick. Then she looked out the window as if she were expecting someone.

"You'll love Jesse," Lori continued. "So, Sara, drop Mickey off at Bunkhouse 13 and check in with Cookie at the chuck wagon."

Sara nodded woodenly. A bull rider serving a sentence… She couldn't wait to meet this guy.

Chapter 2

"I know Judge Connor sentenced me to Camp Care, but it's cruel and unusual punishment. It's not cruel and unusual to me, you understand, but to the kids."

Lori grinned from ear to ear. She was so easy to flirt with. "And not that I'm superstitious, but Bunkhouse 13 is a little ironic, isn't it? But why don't you just call it Bunkhouse *Titanic*?"

Lori tilted her head and twirled a brown curl. "You'll be wonderful, Jesse. Just be yourself."

"Be myself? Okay. I ride bulls. I'll go into Bunkhouse 13 for eight seconds. Then I'll hit the ground and run away."

She laughed loudly.

Her eyes twinkled. "The psychiatrists, counselors, therapists and psychologists on our staff can help you. That's what they do."

"Oh, yes. They are in that nice house that looks like a bank. Meantime, I'm in a bunkhouse that was built in 1860."

"Jesse, you're a hoot." Lori chuckled. "And guess who's monitoring your community service and reporting back to Judge Connor?"

"You?"

"At your service, cowboy."

Out of the corner of his eye, Jesse saw a woman enter with a young boy. Maybe the kid was about nine or ten.

Lori cleared her throat. "Hold that thought, Jesse. I'm going to see what Mrs. Peterson needs." She turned to Sara. "Is there something else, Mrs. Peterson?"

"I need directions to the chuck wagon and Mickey's cabin. I checked the map but I couldn't find either one."

Lori pointed to the map. "Oh, see? It's right here. It's in the shape of a big chuck wagon…sort of," Lori said, giggling. "We changed the facade on it to look like a chuck wagon after those flyers were printed. But I guess you have to use your imagination."

"Mickey's cabin is right next to the chuck wagon. That's terrific. I can keep an eye on him." Sara turned to Jesse and raised an eyebrow.

"Oh, where are my manners?" Lori said. "Sara Peterson, I'd like you to meet Jesse Beaumont. He's going to be Mickey's ramrod. And this is Mickey. Mickey, this is Mr. Beaumont. Sara and Mickey live in Henderson Falls, near Syracuse, New York."

Sara ignored Jesse's outstretched hand and turned to Lori.

Ouch, that hurt. *Nothing like a complete snub.*

"I am going to go out on the deck and talk to Jesse. Then, Lori, the three of us need to have a conversation."

Sara Peterson might be even better looking if her blond hair wasn't pulled back into such a tight bun at the nape of her neck. Maybe she had a nice smile, but he hadn't seen evidence of one at all.

To top it all off, she was bossy.

Sara shook her head. "I'm sorry, but based on what I've overheard, I've reconsidered placing Mickey in your program." She took a deep breath. "Are all your staff defendants serving a sentence here?"

"Jesse's the only one. Community service, you know."

"That…cowboy…is a defendant?" she asked, eyes narrowed.

Lori grinned. "Uh…um…technically, yes, but he'll be great."

Jesse raised an eyebrow. "Uh, he's standing right here."

"And he's going to be responsible for my Mickey? To help him get better?" Sara asked, clearly disgusted.

"Sure," Lori said.

"Um…why don't you ask *him*?" Jesse shifted his stance. "He's been standing here listening."

She looked shocked as if Jesse had just entered the room. Suddenly, her face softened, and she turned to Jesse.

"I'm sorry, Mr. Beaumont, but I can't help how I feel. I don't trust a lot of people with Mickey. Lori, please, just please, find Mickey another bunkhouse with a ramrod who is not a criminal and who has had some experience dealing with kids like him."

Darn it all. He resented being called a criminal and was irritated with the woman. She didn't even know him. Shoot. It probably would be worth it to just to do his time in jail and watch this place disappear in his rearview mirror.

"Lori," Jesse moved toward the door. "This lady doesn't want a criminal taking care of her kid, and probably the other parents think the same way, so, Lori, please tell Judge Connor that Jesse Beaumont should hit the trail," he said, keeping with the Western theme.

Lori tapped the counter with a pen. "Can't do it, Jesse. The judge said that you'd try to worm out of your sentence. He said to tell you each time to quit whining and get to work. He said that no one is better with horses than you, and he has faith in your ability to work with kids."

"Dam...darn him!"

"He also said that you'd try and pick me up."

At that remark, Jesse couldn't help but let loose a loud belly laugh. Poor Sara Peterson jumped a foot at his sound. So did her son.

Jesse turned toward Sara, who had her hand on the doorknob, seemingly ready to escape. "Mrs. Peterson, it appears that I'm stuck here for a while. If nothing else, I *am* great with bulls and horses. I won't let your kid fall off a horse if that's what you're worried about, and I won't corrupt him."

Sara looked from Lori to Jesse. She was going to lose this one. "Please step outside, Mr. Beaumont. I'd like to speak with you in private."

He leaned down to Mickey and winked. "I hope your mom isn't going to beat me up."

The boy blinked, but not much else. Poor kid. Jesse wondered why Mickey didn't talk, didn't react.

Sara Peterson was waiting for him on the deck. This wasn't going to be good.

She crossed her arms as he closed the office door and stood across from her. "Go ahead, Mrs. Peterson."

"One more time, Mr. Beaumont, I don't want to offend you, but I don't want a criminal in charge of my son. I don't want him to be my son's ramrod or camp counselor or whatever you're to be called."

"Call me Jesse."

"*Mr. Beaumont*, there's a lot at stake here. I think that my money is best spent elsewhere."

Suddenly, Jesse decided to put his objections aside and do his best.

"Bull! This is a great program. I've heard that there have been a lot of success stories as a result of the kids staying here, and kids who started out not speaking left chattering away." That he did know. "Mickey could be one of them. Give him a chance."

Sara uncrossed her arms, but looked ready to pounce on him.

He took a deep breath and let it out. "Look, Mrs.

Peterson, please keep Mickey in the program, and I'll do my best not to be a criminal. Okay?"

"I should ask you what you *did* to become a criminal."

"It's a long story. I was in the wrong place at the wrong time."

"As was every criminal before you."

"No. Really. And if I satisfactorily ramrod the kids and wrangle the horses for the month—or is it the other way around?—my arrest will be expunged."

"So what did you do?" Sara asked. "Give me the short version."

"My crime was disorderly conduct—a fight in the parking lot of a bar after a rodeo. It was bull riders versus bronc riders, and I'm proud to say that the bull riders won. It's not the crime of the century, but I hope I eased your mind."

"You did somewhat ease my mind, Mr. Beaumont."

"Jesse."

"*Mr. Beaumont*, I'll give you a small period of time to see how you are doing with my son. If you're not performing to my satisfaction, I'll pull Mickey from the program or get him another…ramrod. I'll be watching you from the kitchen—I mean the *chuck wagon*—where I'll be working. Working there, I can see what Mickey eats, too."

She sounds just like Mrs. Flanagan, my fourth-grade teacher!

When she wasn't bossy and overbearing, Sara Peterson was probably a looker, but Jesse found it difficult to get past her attitude. But perhaps Mickey's silence came from losing a parent.

He could understand that.

"I wanted to discuss something with you. Mickey seems to have a lot of food allergies," he stated.

"What do you mean, Mr. Beaumont?"

"I was reading the folders of my wranglers, and Mickey had quite the list. Can he really be allergic to candy and all other sweets? That's the pits, the poor little wrangler!"

Jesse continued. "You ought to give your kid a break and leave him alone for a while. It's camp, for heaven's sake. This is going to be the Land of the S'mores around the campfire. I'd hate to tell Mickey that he can't have any."

"I just want him to eat healthy." Her eyes sparked like his backfiring old Ford pickup.

"He will. With some fun stuff thrown in."

Sara ground her foot into the dirt like a mad bull. "Where did you get your degree, Mr. Beaumont?"

"Jesse." He grinned. "I joined the Professional Bull Riders when I was eighteen. Although I have been chipping away at an associate's degree during the summer when the PBR is on break. This summer, my classes are on hold."

"Chipping away?" She fingered her bun, tucking in loose hair. "Chipping away? On what? Child psychology?"

"Animal husbandry and ranch management."

"That certainly doesn't qualify you to take care of my son, does it?"

"Lady, there are psychologists, certified instructors and many more professionals on staff. I am not a certified equine therapist, but we have those that are with many degrees and initials after their names."

"Thank goodness they aren't chipping away at their degrees."

Jesse let out a long whistle. "How about you, Mrs. Peterson? Child psychology?"

"I started working at eighteen," she said quietly, looking down as if she were embarrassed.

What a jerk he was. He didn't mean to humiliate her.

"Look, Mrs. Peterson, like I said, I never professed to be a counselor or a shrink. But kids relate to me, maybe it's because I'm a bull rider and kids like sports players. How do I know? All I know is that I'm going to be in charge of Bunkhouse 13 and the equine program, and I won't let your kid or any kid fail. Is that plain enough, Mrs. Flanagan?"

"Who?"

"I mean, Mrs. Peterson. Sorry, I had you mixed up with someone else for a moment."

She stared up at the sky, then raised her hands as if she was giving up. "Oh, just call me Sara."

"Someday." He tweaked his hat. "Now if you'll excuse me, I have my wranglers to meet and greet and enjoy some bag lunches." He turned to leave, then snapped his fingers. "Oh, and Mrs. Peterson, please make sure you bring Mickey to Bunkhouse 13 as soon as possible. I'd like him to get acquainted with his fellow campers, or wranglers, all seven of them, plus me."

* * *

As Sara walked from the deck back into the office to claim Mickey, she fumed. Jesse Beaumont had some nerve to talk to her like he had.

Merciful heavens! He even admitted that he was "chipping away at an associate's degree." He didn't seem to have any experience in dealing with children in need, and his only claim to fame was being a bull rider and having some experience with horses.

"I should have told him that bull riding isn't a big deal in central New York like it is out West," Sara mumbled under her breath as she went to the Assay Office to pick up Mickey. "I am not impressed in the least with Jesse Beaumont."

She had to admit that her heart skipped a few beats when Jesse looked at her. She must be jet-lagged, thinking along those lines. She'd been thinking that he was a handsome guy, even when she was questioning his credentials. That jet-black hair and piercing blue eyes made her knees buckle and her heart beat so fast, she thought it was going to jump out of her chest. Admittedly, her judgment was skewed. After all, she'd picked Mr. Good Time, Michael Peterson, to marry eleven years ago.

She figured that she got pregnant with Mickey on their first Christmas together because Michael's favorite sports bar was closed.

It had been a while before she figured out that most of Michael's affable personality resulted from hanging with his drinking buddies rather than being content with her and Mickey at home. Michael probably only managed to keep his job as a supervisor at an automobile assembly line because he never appeared intoxicated at work, and because he could talk his way out of any trouble, but after work, he never came right home, not even after Michael Jr. was born. Instead, he headed for Finley's Sports Bar, and its endlessly flowing green beer, while she stayed and home and raised their son.

In spite of resenting Michael, she'd stuck it out for Mickey's sake, and look what had happened. What a fool.

Entering the assay's office again, she saw Mickey sitting inside, staring out the side window. Usually, he stayed where she left him and didn't move. But Lori must have taken his hand and showed him something out the window. She glanced out the window to see what he was looking at. It was Bunkhouse 13.

"Mickey, are you ready to get settled into your bunkhouse and meet some new friends?" Lori asked from behind her desk.

Mickey walked toward her. To Sara, that showed an overwhelming amount of interest on his part. Usually, if someone didn't physically touch him to get his attention, he'd stay in his own world forever.

It had all started with the accident. Her husband had been driving with Mickey in the car, talking on his cell phone, when he collided with a bridge piling. For once he hadn't been drinking.

Michael died on the spot, and remarkably, their beautiful boy was unscathed physically. But he had not spoken another word since the accident and had sleepwalked through life in his own little world.

It didn't surprise her that Mickey was diagnosed with selective mutism and PTSD: Post-Traumatic Stress Disorder. And if anyone had the right to be under stress, it was Mickey.

Tears sprang to Sara's eyes, but she quickly brushed them away so Mickey wouldn't see them. Her son got upset when she cried and would hide his head. Yes, she was going to remain positive with Mickey.

In spite of her difficulties with Jesse Beaumont, she was going to hope for the best. Maybe she'd be pleasantly surprised.

If it didn't work out, she'd be back to talk to Lori.

"See you two later at dinner." Lori waved. "Today's lunch is sandwiches, milk and cookies. Because it's moving-in day and the kids come in various times, bag lunches are in the little fridge by the ramrod's desk."

Sara nodded. "Goodbye, Lori. I'll check in at the kitchen—I mean, chuck wagon—as soon as I get Mickey settled in his cabin—I mean, bunkhouse." She took Mickey's hand and led him out of the room, onto the deck and down the stairs. Then they walked to number thirteen.

Jesse came jogging toward them. "Lady, let go of Mickey's hand! This isn't the first day of kindergarten. The other kids will pick on him forever, if they see that. Do you want him to fail before he starts?"

Sara had a feeling that Jesse might be right in this instance, so she turned to Mickey. "Okay?"

Of course Mickey didn't answer, but stared at Jesse.

"Look, why don't you go and get Mickey's gear bag, and I'll get him settled."

"Gear bag? You mean suitcase?"

He rolled his eyes. "What does it look like?"

"It's white. With a skyline of New York City on it in black."

Jesse took her by the elbow and moved her away from Mickey, then turned to the boy. "Hang on for a second, Mickey, and I'll get your lunch. I have to speak to your mother."

He took her aside and whispered, "For Pete's sake! Mickey will be beat up before he steps a foot on the dusty wooden floor."

"Dusty? My son is allergic to dust."

"Then take him to the Ritz. It's down the street, take a left."

"Is there a Ritz—"

"Of course not!" Jesse pushed his cowboy hat back with a thumb. "Let's get back to the suitcase problem." He pulled a set of keys from the pocket of his jeans, singled out one, and handed it to her. "In the back seat of the black pickup over there—" He pointed to the first truck in the first row. "There's an empty brown duffel with the PBR logo on it. Take Mickey's stuff out of that suitcase of yours and put his gear in the PBR duffel. I promise you, he'll be the biggest hit of Bunkhouse 13—that is, after me, of course."

"Oh, absolutely, Mr. Beaumont. There's nothing conceited about you."

"Not a thing," Jesse said. "Take your time. Let me introduce Mickey to the other seven wranglers before his momma comes back."

Jesse motioned for Mickey to follow him, and the kid did so, with just a glance as to where his mother was going. He opened his small fridge that had contained nine bag lunches. Now, with Mickey's arrival, all were gone.

"Your mom is getting you one of my gear bags and is switching your stuff into it. That one you have is a little too much on the mom side. We cowboys don't put our stuff into luggage. Right, Mickey? From now on, you're toting your gear in a PBR duffel. You'll be the hit of Bunkhouse 13."

He wasn't positive, but it seemed that there was a light in the child's eyes that wasn't there before, but it was gone as soon as it appeared.

Jesse opened the bunkhouse door for Mickey, but the boy hesitated. "I got your back," Jesse said, and he heard Mickey let out a deep breath.

The boy went through the door, but just barely. Jesse had to gently nudge him to go farther into the bunkhouse.

"Wranglers, I'd like you all to meet the eighth wrangler of Bunkhouse 13, Mickey Peterson. He's going to take the last bunk, the one under the window." Jesse made eye contact with Mickey, then pointed to his bed. "Please make Mickey welcome."

"Howdy!" someone yelled. There was some clapping from those who didn't speak.

There was no reaction from Mickey.

"Yo, dude, you should at least wave at your bunk-mates. They're saying hi. You need to say hi back to them," Jesse said.

Mickey gave a quick wave, which seemed to satisfy the other boys. Everyone went back to what they were doing, which was mostly unpacking and putting their gear into the two-drawer wooden dressers in between the bunks.

There was a knock on the cabin door. *Sara.* Entering, she carried in the PBR duffel bag and stood next to Jesse. He gave her a nod, took the duffel from her, then turned to Mickey, and said in a loud voice. "That must be your gear, Mickey. Hey, nice bag! I have a PBR duffel just like that one."

Along with Mickey, all the boys gathered around the bag, looking at the big PBR logo.

"Wow," said Steve, a boy with dark curly hair and dark features. He walked on prosthetic legs. He was hugging a package of crew socks that he hadn't put away yet. "Dude, that is major cool."

"Yeehaw!" said Brendon, a tall, thin boy with shocking red hair and ears that could fly. He had muscular dystrophy. So did Jackson, a pale boy on the shy side.

"This-s is-s so c-cool," said David.

Ty, J.B., Mickey and Glen were nonverbal, but they nodded.

Brendon said, "I watch bull riding and rodeo on TV, and we have the coolest ramrod at Camp Care—a real bull rider."

Jesse pumped the air with a fist. "You know it! Go Bunkhouse 13!" He heard only four voices cheering, excluding his. He vowed to change that. He wanted eight voices cheering. Sure, he was aiming for a perfect score, but he was bound and determined to try like hell to achieve one. "Now, wranglers, finish unpacking. I have to talk to Mickey's mother for a second."

Jesse opened the door for her and they went outside.

"What do you think?" he asked.

She didn't speak for several seconds. "Okay, you were right about the duffel bag."

"Can I have that in writing?"

"No way." She smiled and her whole face lit up. She should do that more often; it made her green eyes shine like twin emeralds. How come he hadn't noticed them before?

"Then how about a moonlight walk around the grounds?" he asked. "The wranglers will be at the campfire, according to my schedule."

"I don't think so," Sara said. "I'm not one of your teeny boppers."

"They're called buckle bunnies."

"Whatever. But I'd bet you enjoy the attention."

He winked. "Enjoy? What do you mean by that?"

"Lori Floyd, for one. I'm sure you're used to women flirting with you."

Jesse winked. "All the time." He didn't know why he was teasing her, but he liked how she sparred with him. With all the buckle bunnies hanging around him and the rest of the bull riders, Jesse wasn't used to women challenging him like Sara did. He kind of liked it.

"Look, Mr. Beaumont, let's change the subject."

"What did I do now, Mrs. Peterson?"

"You assigned Mickey to the window bunk, and he has allergies, and I don't want him to get cold at night."

"The fresh air will be good for him, and he can always shut the window. I'm sure he knows how to do that. And there's a box of tissues on the dresser between each bunk. Does he take allergy meds? I don't remember seeing that in his folder."

"No, but I have a box of them in my purse."

"Over-the-counter?"

"Yes," she replied, her eyes meeting his as if ready for another battle.

"Not allowed," he said simply. "Wranglers must go to the camp doctor for anything like that."

"I suppose that's all okay." She looked at her map. "At least if he needs me, I'm not far away."

"I'm sure you don't want Mickey treated any different than the other five wranglers whose mothers aren't here. Right?"

"But I *am* here, Mr. Beaumont."

"Mrs. Peterson, please, give him some room."

She rolled her eyes. "Is that your professional advice?"

"Nope. It's my gut feeling."

"What else does your gut tell you?" she asked.

"That you have to relax, and I'm just the cowboy to show you how."

Chapter 3

A half hour later, Sara seethed as she walked over to the chuck wagon with Mickey. At least the bull rider let Mickey out of Bunkhouse 13 to grab some lunch with her, since he wasn't a fan of bologna and cheese. But she had to take another child with her—Ty was the boy's name. He wasn't a fan of bologna sandwiches, either.

Jesse made it clear that from now on, they would eat what they were given. But that was nice of him, for now.

Not that she was softening toward Jesse. The bull rider had a lot of nerve analyzing her and telling her what to do.

Relax, he'd said.

As if she hadn't tried to. She'd tried meditating,

yoga, power walking and taking a nap on the weekends. Nothing worked because she couldn't quiet her mind.

Sara thought she knew what Mickey needed, and that was this camp. It sounded therapeutic, and yet fun. Besides, Camp Care came highly recommended by Mickey's school psychologist, so she'd put all her hope and prayers that something—someone—here would be able to reach her son.

She'd even sunk every cent she had, even lost her job, in the hope that Mickey would respond.

And what did Mickey get? A bull rider with "gut feelings." And one of those gut feelings pertained to her parenting!

She had too much at stake. Mickey needed to be in another bunkhouse.

Sara vowed to facilitate Mickey's transfer, but now it was time to concentrate on her scholarship job.

She studied the kitchen as she approached. If she used her imagination, she could see the back end of a chuck wagon to the right of the door. There were fairly authentic tin cans and metal utensils hanging from various nooks and crannies of the chuck wagon.

She opened the door and was greeted by a bear of a man. "Welcome to Camp Care's Chuck Wagon! What can I get you?"

"I'm Sara Peterson, and I'm assigned to work here to pay off part of my son's fee."

"And I'm Phil Stillwell." He extended a meaty hand and Sara shook it. Phil had such a strong grip, she thought that her fingers would never work again. "But they call me Cookie. In fact, every chuck wagon that ever hit the trail had a Cookie, no matter what their real name was."

"Then 'Cookie' it will be." Sara liked him immediately.

"And who are these wranglers?"

"This is my son, Mickey Peterson, and this is Ty. They are both new wranglers."

"Excellent!" Phil's booming voice echoed through the huge hall. "Who's their ramrod?"

"Jesse Beaumont."

"Outstanding! We are happy to have all of you here," Phil shouted, then lowered his voice. "Lori called me and said that you'd be coming over for chow. Lunch is over, but I cooked up some hot dogs and beans. Doesn't that sound like a cowboy meal, hey, Mickey? Ty?"

No answer. But both boys followed Phil with his eyes. That at least was some kind of reaction.

"We'd love lunch," Sara said.

Phil pointed to the front of the room. "Help yourself to drinks and take a seat. Then we'll talk about your duties. Okay? I'll be right back."

After Phil left, Sara looked around the dining hall. The hangings on the wall were more cooking implements and big poster-size pictures of authentic chuck wagons of old. Sara turned to the two boys. "I think this is going to be a fun place for you wranglers."

By the time Sara got three iced teas, Phil returned,

and was setting three heaping plates of beans and two hot dogs in front of them.

Mickey started eating immediately. He must be hungry—so was Sara—though Ty waited a few minutes.

Phil slapped his palms on the table, and the three of them jumped. "I suppose you'd like to know what your duties will be."

"Yes. I would."

"Eat! Eat! We can talk while you're eating." He grinned. "Well, Sara, you'll be doing everything from preparing meals to dishing them out on the assembly line, and then cleaning up afterward. The kids and the ramrods will take their trays to the table over there, clean everything off, and place the dishes and such in the gray bins. Then you will take over and feed the dishwasher."

"And this is for every meal?" she asked.

"Yes, Sara. It's not as bad as it sounds, and you'll have help. I have others whose kids are on scholarships assigned to work here."

"Oh, I don't think it's bad at all. When do I start?" she asked.

"Come back at about four o'clock. We eat at five. It'll be chaos with the new wranglers and ramrods and everyone getting to know one another and them getting to know us, but I guarantee you that it'll be fun. Now finish your chow and put your dishes and trays over there." He pointed to the back of the room.

He held out his hand, and Sara took it. "See you

later, Sara. And, Mickey and Ty, you wranglers have a great time at the Double C."

Sara nodded. "See you later, Cookie."

They finished their "chow" and put their trays where Cookie instructed. Sara couldn't help but laugh as she and Mickey and Ty walked down the stairs of the chuck wagon. The food was actually good.

She had a warm feeling that this was going to be a fun job. She was just hoping that Mickey and his fellow wranglers would enjoy their experiences, too.

Having fun was fine, but she wanted Mickey to benefit from the fun.

But she'd like to help in the kitchen as much as she was able. When she saw a menu, she could suggest changes to the cowboy grub to make it a bit healthier for Mickey and everyone else. She liked to cook and liked to experiment with herbs and spices. She smiled; wait until the bull rider heard about her plan!

Ahead and to the right of the chuck wagon, she could see Jesse Beaumont sitting on a large log. He was surrounded by most of the kids from Bunkhouse 13, who were also sitting on logs.

She reminded herself that it was a plus that Bunkhouse 13 was right next to the chuck wagon. She could observe both Mickey and Jesse, and note any progress, or lack thereof.

Jesse waved Mickey and Ty over, and both boys slowly walked toward the gathering. The other boys moved over for them to take a seat.

Sara slowed her pace as she walked by the gathering on the way to her bunkhouse.

"Real cowboys live by the Cowboy Code. The Cowboy Code is rules for living. For instance, you should never pass anyone on the trail without saying 'Howdy.' Oh, and if you complain about the cooking, you'd better be prepared to be the Cookie. And honesty is gold. Your word is your bond, and a handshake is more binding than a contract. And speaking of gold, always live by the Golden Rule—'Do unto others as you would have them do unto you.' A cowboy's job is never done. Kindness and respect are what makes a cowboy a cowboy. There's more, but we'll take them a couple at a time, right here, every day, and talk about each one."

Judging by the glow on her son's face, he felt as if he'd just been handed the Ten Commandments by Moses on Mount Sinai. The other campers looked just as riveted.

Okay, so maybe Jesse the Ramrod would be okay after all. The Cowboy Code had a lot of merit, and the boys would benefit from knowing it.

Sara grudgingly admitted to herself that she'd developed some respect for Jesse. Not only was he presenting good rules for living, but he was also telling the wranglers of Bunkhouse 13 what he expected of them.

Ingenious ramrod!

Maybe not.

Sara picked up speed and walked to the Cowgirls'

Bunkhouse, Number 16, which Lori had circled on the map with a big "Sara's Bunkhouse" in red.

Stopping at her car, she picked up her two suitcases, both of which had the theme of the New York City skyline. She could understand how Mickey would have been mocked by the kids, after Jesse pointed it out to her. Mickey could have indicated that he didn't want to bring the suitcase to Camp Care, but that would have required some type of communication, and that wasn't Mickey.

Rolling her two suitcases on the dirt walkway, she headed to the stairs of Bunkhouse 16. As she got closer, she could hear the laughter coming out the open windows. With her hand on the doorknob, she paused. She hadn't been camping since seventh grade, and she remembered rows of bunk beds in a dozen big green buildings at Pine Crest Camp. There, the mattresses were thin and the walls were unfinished plywood, loaded with graffiti like "Carly slept here" and "Annie loves Jake."

She smiled, remembering good times and a lot of laughs. She'd met a lot of girls who promised "friendship forever" when their two weeks ended. Eventually, as the years passed by, those promises faded.

Now, she was even more isolated. It had been two years. Two years of silence with Mickey and giving him her every waking moment. Before that, it was nine years of marriage with Michael, a nearly sexless, but semi-companionable, marriage.

After Michael died in the accident, and Mickey

became nonverbal, she became focused on helping her son.

She didn't have time for much else.

A couple of guys she'd met at church had asked her out, but she'd turned them down. She was too tired to work at a relationship and too tired to go out. It was probably a mistake to shut them out—she should date and enjoy herself—but she couldn't manage the energy or interest.

But friends she needed.

Sara wished that both she and Mickey would find those here at Camp Care.

Opening the door, she took a breath and stepped inside. She bit back a laugh because it was almost an exact replica of her cabin at Pine Crest Camp. Several women were sitting on their bunks and talking. Two of them approached her and gave her big hugs of welcome. They whisked her away to the group, and everyone introduced themselves.

They were all fellow moms. Three of their children were on scholarship, and they all were workers at the camp.

Sara felt lighter. She could tell that this was going to be fun.

"We were just talking about the hunky ramrod in Bunkhouse 13. We hear he's a bull rider and a real cowboy," said Julia, who had said that she'd be working at the chuck wagon, too. "I wonder what his name is."

"Those blue eyes...yum!"

"Just like turquoise."

"I wonder if he's married."

"I don't think so," Sara said. She didn't want to tell the group that he'd been chastising her. "And his name is Jesse Beaumont."

Julia snapped her fingers. "I thought he looked familiar. He's one of the Beaumont Big Guns, the three brothers who are in the top three spots on the Professional Bull Riders standings on the circuit."

Another woman who'd introduced herself as Maggie added, "They are the favorites to win the five-day PBR Finals in Las Vegas this year. Only no one can decide which brother will actually win it."

Sara couldn't care less if he won or lost the bull riding finals. She didn't even know if she wanted to get to know him. He'd judged her parenting skills and found her wanting.

After all, what did he know? He should walk a mile in her sandals.

Sara picked a top bunk that had a direct view of Bunkhouse 13. She told herself that it might be fun to sleep up in the air, but to be honest, she could watch Mickey day and night from her position in front of the window.

She wondered what Ramrod Jesse would have to say about that.

Yes, Ramrod Jesse. Handsome beyond belief. His arms bulged with muscles, and he had a tan that was probably from hard work on his ranch. His lips were made for kissing. Yes, he was a cowboy through and through.

What was she doing thinking about him romantically? She didn't need a man in her life. Men changed personality after the statement: "I now pronounce you husband and wife."

Adding to the chatter now and then, she unpacked and put her things in the small dresser that was provided between each bunk. Then she made her bed, which was no easy task. She wasn't short by any means, but the bunk was really high.

"Sara, we'd better get up to the chuck wagon for dinner soon. Phil wants us there an hour early. I wonder what the menu is tonight," Julia said.

"Phil didn't tell me," Sara replied.

"It's more likely that we'll be the ones doing the cooking as the days go on," Julia said. "This isn't my first time here."

"As they say, it's not your first rodeo!" Sara quipped.

Both women laughed. "We are going to have fun in the kitchen," Julia said. "And maybe Jesse Beaumont and I can talk a little and get to know one another."

Sara nodded. "Fingers crossed for you."

Jesse got a kick out of the kids—or should he say the wranglers. They were so serious when he was discussing the Cowboy Code. He purposely left out some of the rules meant for older cowboys, but the majority of the code pertained to everyone.

He chuckled when he thought about their subsequent conversation about the Golden Rule. The conversation morphed to the art of spitting and burping.

Was he ever that young?

Jesse got up from his place on the fallen log and felt every bone in his body ache. For someone who was twenty-four, he felt ancient. Bull riding was tough on the body.

As the wranglers went back to the bunkhouse to finish unpacking and to get to know one another, Jesse did some stretching exercises and, once he was feeling better, decided to do some push-ups to strengthen his arms.

His right arm anchored him to the bull when it bucked, so it had to be strong.

The sun was hot, so he got rid of his shirt. He began counting. A couple of hundred push-ups would do it while the kids were in a scheduled break in the bunkhouse. Then they'd have to line up for dinner by the flagpole.

In the neighborhood of fifty push-ups, he saw two women out of the corner of his eye. One was Sara Peterson who was trying to be aloof, the other had her mouth open and was visibly ogling him.

Jesse winked. "Hi, ladies. Just doing a little exercise while the wranglers are taking a break. Would you like to do them with me?"

Julia found her voice first. "No, thanks. I couldn't keep up. I'd rather watch."

Jesse stopped and slipped back into his shirt.

Julia pulled at Sara's sleeve. "Too bad he put his shirt on, huh, Sara? I was enjoying watching him. He's amazingly fit."

When he put his shirt, it was like covering up a Picasso. She blinked to get back to reality. Reality was a mute son; fantasizing about this bull rider wasn't for her. Jesse was nice to look at, but that was about it.

"Julia, you go ahead to the chuck wagon. I'll be right there," Sara said. "I'd like to speak with Mr. Beaumont for a second."

Julia gasped as if Sara had just told her that she was going to have a meeting with the Pope. "What? Really? Okay, sure."

Sara waited until Julia was almost to the chuck wagon, then she turned to Jesse. "I couldn't help overhearing what you said to the kids about the Cowboy Code. They were paying absolute attention to every word you were saying. Mickey was enthralled, too."

"I noticed Mickey," Jesse said. "It was as if he were hypnotized."

"They all were. You're reaching them. Mickey doesn't look that way at me when I'm speaking."

"You're his mother. I'm someone different and a sports figure. That's why."

Sara shrugged. "You're right." She looked around and shifted on her feet. She should apologize to him for their earlier discussion, but she wasn't ready to surrender the sting of his know-it-all comments. "Well, I'd better get going. I don't want to be late my first day on the job," she said.

"Same here." Jesse buttoned the top button of his shirt. "I'd better get my wranglers ready for chow. See you at the chuck wagon."

Sara entered the chuck wagon's door, glanced at the rows of long tables and folding chairs, which wouldn't be empty for long, and went in back to the kitchen to find Phil.

He was talking to Julia. "Hi, Sara. I understand you already met Julia."

"Please, everyone call me Jules," she said. "And we know each other," she said to Phil.

"Good." Phil handed Sara a white chef's apron and Jules helped her tie it in the back.

"Thanks," Sara said.

Phil pointed. "Sara, you and Jules will be at the steam table. Everyone will come through with trays and plates. Sara will dish out the spaghetti. Jules, you ladle out sauce and two meatballs. The ramrods get three meatballs," Phil said. "Rolls and butter will be on the table, along with a bowl of family-style salad. Our other helper, my wife, Margie, will take care of that stuff."

"I'll keep your steam tables stocked. I figure that I'll have to refill it all at least twice and once again for second helpings." Cookie grinned. "And it's as simple as that."

"It does sound simple," Sara said. "What aren't you telling us?"

"The noise is unbelievable. You won't be able to hear yourselves think."

No wonder Phil had developed such a booming voice. She'd like nothing better than to hear Mickey make noise, so that wasn't a problem, as far as she was concerned.

"What else?" Jules asked.

"If there's a food fight, make sure you duck, and hurry into the kitchen."

"They wouldn't dare," Sara said.

Jules chuckled. "It happens at least once a session. The little kids are the worst. And Phil makes everyone wash the walls and clean it all up. No exceptions."

"Good. No one should waste food." Sara thought about how there were times when she didn't have much money for food, and how she could make soup or stew out of nothing. Wasting food should be a violation of the…the…Cowboy Code at least!

She could hear a nondenominational prayer being said by Lori Floyd over the loudspeaker. "…and help us to live by the Cowboy Code and live by the Golden Rule. Help us to be kind to everyone we meet. Help us to enjoy our time at Camp Care and have some fun. Amen."

"Amen," echoed most everyone.

The bunkhouses were called in numerical order. Lori explained that later they would call out bunkhouses by cleanliness; Bunkhouse 13 was the last to be called.

The doors flew open and the wranglers headed for trays and plates. Margie had already set the tables with salad and rolls and set out pitchers of water, milk and iced tea.

The wranglers headed for Sara at a dead run, but she held her ground like Stonewall Jackson. She picked up hot spaghetti with a pair of tongs and set it on plate after plate as they came sliding in front of her. She almost missed Mickey when he came by, but he clinked his spoon against his plate for her to notice him.

Sara was shocked and jubilant at the same time. Normally, her son wouldn't call attention to himself in any way. This was a big deal to her, and Mickey hadn't even been at Camp Care for a whole day. "Mickey! How are you?"

He nodded.

He *nodded*!

Mickey had to move to Jules's station for his meatballs before the other wranglers physically pushed him along, so when Jesse Beaumont appeared at the steam table she was wiping tears from her eyes with the bottom of her apron.

Rarely did Mickey communicate when he was asked a question, and he never looked into her eyes. Never. "Mrs. Peterson, what's wrong?" Jesse's turquoise eyes were full of concern. "Are you hurt? Did you burn yourself?" He came around the table to where she was standing and took her hands in his. He inspected them, front and back.

"Shh…" She whispered in his ear, enjoying his smell of pine and cedar. She didn't want Mickey or Jules to hear. "I'll tell you later. But it's a happy cry."

"Oh, one of those." Jesse winked. "My mother used to have happy cries all the time."

Jesse got back in line, and Sara gave him the biggest portion of spaghetti that she could. Turning to

Jules, she said, "Don't forget the extra meatball for the ramrods."

"This ramrod deserves four meatballs," Jules said, then giggled.

"Thanks, ma'am," Jesse reached to tweak his hat, but he wasn't wearing one. He nodded instead, then moved on.

"That man is just gorgeous," Jules whispered to Sara. "Are you two an item?"

"An item?" Sara gritted her teeth. "No. He's not my type."

But what *was* her type?

Her husband, Michael, had been more interested in the local bars instead. Before the bars opened, he was more enchanted with his reference books that listed car parts than he was in being with her and Mickey.

Sharpening pencils was the extent of his exercise. His black Dodge truck was his reward for a job well done from his company. If Michael could have worked twenty-four hours a day, seven days a week, instead of coming home to them, he would have.

At least he'd supported them. Mickey hadn't wanted for anything, and Sara hadn't wanted anything from Michael.

As she sweated over the spaghetti, Sara wondered what Michael would think if he saw her now, working for tuition. He'd always wanted her to be more of a showpiece, the perfect wife and mother who entertained his supervisors with dinner parties, so his well-heeled bosses might promote him even higher.

They'd grown apart almost immediately after Mickey was born. Mickey had come as a surprise to them both, but even more to Michael, who would have rather done anything than hang with his own son. Sara supposed that Michael loved their child in his own way, but he never showed that to Mickey.

Then the accident happened. Michael had picked up Mickey from hockey practice as planned, when he got a phone call from one of his workers on the assembly line that the line had gone down.

Michael had answered it, talked for a while, went through a red light and hit that bridge piling. Michael died, and Mickey had not spoken or cried in the two years since. It was as if Mickey was punishing himself.

In those two years, she took Mickey to at least four psychiatrists. He saw school counselors and school psychologist in between. They'd all exchanged notes on Mickey, and she read them, too.

Nonverbal.

Won't make eye contact.

In his own world.

PTSD from the accident.

Selective mutism.

Could the bull rider possibly do what the professionals could not?

Chapter 4

Two days later, as Jesse walked down the worn dirt path to the spring-fed mountain lake, he wondered why he suddenly felt unsure of himself with his wranglers.

After he attended a meeting with medical personnel, it hit him for the first time that he'd been roped into a big responsibility.

Eight young lives were suddenly under his care. By the end of the month, Jesse wanted to return them to their families just the way they had been dropped off, at least physically—with no bones broken or bruises. But even more, young minds were so vulnerable; he didn't want to do or say anything that would warp them for life.

Jesse wanted to help improve their minds and help

with their various special needs. After reading their files and taking copious notes, Jesse formulated a plan for each wrangler, and planned to run them by the gang who resided in the fake bank made of bricks, the specialists. His wranglers were very impressionable. Jesse already noticed Glen and J.B. imitating the way he walked, with a little limp in their gait. Six months ago, a bull had gotten a little too frisky with his horns at the Colorado event, and it resulted in a tiny hitch in his own giddyup. It would eventually go away.

Steve and Brendon had already phoned their parents and asked for Wrangler jeans and Resistol hats because that was what Jesse sported.

All his wranglers sported red bandannas around their necks. They were a gift from Jesse on the first day of camp. He thought the boys would like them. One by one they had Jesse autograph the bandannas, and they wore them all day yesterday and today, as if they were some type of symbol of Bunkhouse 13.

Yes, the wranglers in Bunkhouse 13 were bonding. Those who could, talked all night and into the wee hours of the morning. His wranglers even had a burping contest, with the non-talkers winning it. Jesse didn't care if they pulled an all-nighter; he wanted the wranglers to enjoy their stay, but he wondered what Sara Peterson would say.

There would be hell to pay if Mickey didn't get enough sleep and dozed off during lunch onto his tray of chicken soup and a ham and cheese sandwich.

Jesse could see the blue lake through an opening in the conifer trees. The private property belonged to Camp Care. And who owned Camp Care and the lake? None other than Judge Richard Connor and his family, the sidewinder responsible for him being here.

Actually he didn't mind. Ricky had been hounding him to help out at Camp Care for a few years. Jesse's two brothers, Luke and Reed, had already spent a couple of years each as ramrods. It was Jesse's turn, but he didn't even get a chance to volunteer.

He grinned. If he really objected, Ricky would have let him go, but even though he wanted to help his brothers with their houses, that would wait.

The kids of Bunkhouse 13 needed him.

Jesse would love to help Sara, too, if he could. In reading Mickey's file, he figured that she had a hard go of it, both before and after the accident. He was sure that a widow with a young son could use a positive male role model in both of their lives.

But she seemed scared to get involved with him. She was interested, he was sure of that, but wary. She didn't appear to trust him anymore than she had Michael Sr.

He chuckled. Not trust Jesse Beaumont? Why, that was impossible!

He reached the clearing and stood in awe of the pristine lake surrounded by trees. Visible through the water as it gently lapped at the shore were small, colorful stones.

And sitting cross-legged near the shore on a patch of grass was Sara Peterson.

She didn't see him, so he had a chance to observe her.

Her face was turned up to the waning sun, and although her blond hair was in a bun, some strands had gotten loose and stirred in the slight breeze. Sara didn't move, and it appeared that she was either meditating or she had fallen asleep.

He hated to disturb her; she was so calm and peaceful, unlike the Sara Peterson of yesterday who came to the assay office in a thunderstorm of doubt about him and a hurricane of fury about his lack of credentials.

In the evening, when the sun was a blaze of colors as it set, Sara Peterson looked like an ethereal being, a goddess.

"Hey, bull rider, who's watching the kids in Bunkhouse 13?" she said.

A goddess? Have I thrown a horseshoe?
Yes, I must be totally off my gait.

"A roving ramrod is watching the kids," Jesse replied. "I guess there are several who relieve us when we want to take a break."

"You needed a break already?" she asked.

"I needed to take a walk and look at something other than four walls full of graffiti and listening to a bunch of boys having a burping contest."

Sara stood up and did some yoga stretches he recognized from his own routine. He wished he had a camera to capture her surprise when he joined her in her routine.

"A bull rider who does yoga?" she asked, eyes wide.

"A lot of us do yoga. It helps the bones and helps the brain. And when I remember to do some deep breathing before the chute gate opens and my bull comes bucking out, that helps, too."

"I can see where yoga and deep breathing would help you with your—"

He sat down on the patch of grass, and to his surprise, she sat down next to him.

"Riding. They help me with my riding. Remember? I'm a bull rider. You remind me of that often."

"I imagine you have to love it, or you'd get another job. Maybe in an office."

"That's not for me, Sara. Not a chance. I'd starve first. I work at my family's ranch whenever I can with my two brothers, and my father when he's able. It's been in my family since the Oklahoma Land Rush."

"A real ranch?"

He laughed. "A real ranch. Horses, bulls, calves. We rope, brand, vaccinate and ride. We have a bull riding school for new riders, and an equine program for special needs kids that's run by accredited therapists when there's enough kids to participate. A lot of the PBR bull riders help out."

"I think I owe you an apology. You obviously are a qualified cowboy, but you still aren't a qualified therapist."

"Are you referring to your son, who won the burping contest?"

"He what?"

"According to his bunkhouse mates, he was the winner. Everyone owes him a candy bar when the canteen opens."

"Canteen?"

"The store. They get to go three times a week, starting tomorrow. Some money from their tuition goes to an account for them at the canteen."

Sara stared at the lake. It was sparkling with orange highlights from the setting sun. "Mickey doesn't need that much candy. I'll put it aside for him."

"The hell you will!" Jesse took a deep breath. "Sara, don't deny your son his victory. Don't you realize that he was laughing, grinning and interacting with his peers? As sure as the sun is setting right now, Mickey is coming out of his shell."

She crossed her fingers. "I wish."

He could barely hear her, but those two little words held a lot of hope. "And it's only been one day. After the burping contest, there was talk about a farting contest. It's lucky that Mickey has that window next to his bunk now, isn't it? I remember you complaining about it."

She nodded. "I thought about him catching a chill, not about airing out the cabin during a farting contest." She looked into his eyes. "I guess another apology is in order. I seem to be apologizing to you all evening."

"Stop apologizing, then." He held out his hand for a handshake. "Shall we declare a truce?"

She tilted her head. She was clearly thinking about it. "It depends."

"On what?"

"On whether or not you suggested the burping contest."

The laugh burst out from somewhere deep inside of him like a bull busting out of the bucking chute. He never thought that Sara Peterson had the ability to joke, or was she flirting with him?

She held out her hand and he shook it. "I have to admit that I did."

"I knew it!" She laughed. "What more do you have in store for the little wranglers?"

"You'll have to wait and see."

Jesse offered his hand to start back, and she took it, relishing in his warm, calloused fingers that closed over her cool ones, and noticing how little effort it took him to help her up.

As they started back along the path, Sara found herself liking Jesse Beaumont a little bit more. Anyone who does yoga was okay in her book, but more importantly, anyone who could get Mickey Peterson burping and laughing with other wranglers had performed a great miracle.

Sara had first started doing yoga when one of her counselors had suggested it. She knew that she had to do something after the accident to be able to relieve stress.

It was still hard to believe that she lost her husband and part of her son on that day. Her life had changed and she had had to adjust to a new normal, which consisted of many, many counseling appointments for her and Mickey, mostly Mickey.

Some of the appointments were covered by her insurance, partly. She felt that she was working just to pay counselors, psychologists and psychiatrists and none of them accomplished a burping contest to get Mickey laughing and giggling with a budding bunch of friends.

But Jesse had.

She had to chuckle when she thought about how Jesse suggested the burping contest.

Jesse Beaumont was just a kid himself.

No. He was more than that. He could relate to kids. He knew just what made them tick.

And Mickey was enjoying being a kid again.

They reached a fork in the path. Jesse would go left for Bunkhouse 13, and Sara would go right for 16.

But for some reason, she didn't want to leave him just yet. She wanted to ask him more about his bull riding—about anything.

Jesse checked his watch. "I still have some time before the roving ramrod has to rove on, so I'm going to grab a snack at the chuck wagon. Cookie said that there's always something set out for staff. Would you like to join me?"

Sara was hoping that he'd ask. She wasn't ready for the noise and craziness of her bunkmates just yet. If he hadn't asked her, she would have gone alone and further pondered in awe the fact that Mickey won a burping contest over seven other boys.

Mickey successfully interacted with other kids his own age and obviously something about Jesse connected with Mickey. Whatever his motivation, she never knew that her son could win a burping contest.

She was so proud!

Maybe Camp Care was a great idea after all.

"I'd love to join you. I'm not ready to turn in yet," Sara said.

"Great."

They walked straight ahead to the chuck wagon, and Sara shivered. When the sun went down, the temperature plummeted. If she visited the lake at sunset again, she'd have to remember to bring a jacket or sweater.

Jesse immediately pulled his Camp Care sweatshirt over his head, flipped it to the right side, and handed it to Sara. "I'm sorry. Where are my manners?"

"No. I can't take your sweatshirt. I should have brought something…"

He pushed it toward her, and his hands touched hers. Her heart did a silly little flip in her chest that she couldn't explain.

"Put it on. It's getting cold," Jesse said.

Sara hurriedly donned the garment. It was still warm from Jesse's body, and she inhaled his scent. Nice.

She rolled up the cuffs. "Tomorrow I'll bring my own sweatshirt."

"It's a date!" Jesse said quickly.

A date?

"I didn't mean that," she began to explain. "I meant when I do yoga and meditate by the lake, I'll have to remember to bring a sweatshirt."

Jesse grinned. "I knew what you meant. It's a date. I'll meet you by the lake tomorrow night. Same time. Same patch of grass. I'll see if I can get a roving ramrod to cover for me."

"I—I…um… I suppose that's okay."

"Good! And we can continue to get to know each another. Right?"

She shrugged. "I guess so."

He stopped walking. "Gee, Sara, don't sound so excited."

"I haven't dated since the accident."

Sara couldn't fathom why on earth she told Jesse that. It made her sound like such a loser.

"What's wrong with the men in Henderson Falls?" he asked.

"Oh, it's not their fault." She smiled, enjoying their banter. She was getting the hang of it. "I like to stay home with Mickey."

"Maybe you need Camp Care more than Mickey does. Mickey is settling nicely into Bunkhouse 13, so maybe his mom can take a well-deserved break."

She reeled on him just as he opened the door to the chuck wagon for her. "When are you going to quit lecturing me? You don't even know me or my situation."

"Look, Sara, I read and reread my wranglers' folders for Camp Care until I practically memorized them."

She felt his warm hand on the small of her back as he herded her through the door. "Let's finish this conversation inside."

"Let's not finish it at all."

"C'mon, Sara. I'm not your enemy. Let's figure this out, for Mickey's sake."

"Speaking of Mickey, I should make sure that he's wearing his jacket. There's no heat in the cabins."

"Give the kid some space," Jesse suggested.

Sara took a deep breath and walked through the door. She figured that she could take some parenting criticism from the bull rider in exchange for a hot cup of coffee, but not much criticism.

She steeled herself for one of his lectures.

Sara noticed a group of three women in the corner of the chuck wagon, and they all stopped talking and looked up. A couple of giggles escaped, and Sara knew without a doubt that they were talking about Jesse.

She wondered if he knew they were ogling him.

He knew all right. He lifted his hand in a cheerful greeting and grinned. "Hello, ladies. Beautiful evening, isn't it?"

Sara recognized the group as being from her bunkhouse, but its members' names escaped her. She waved, too. "Hi!"

Jesse turned toward her. "Coffee?"

"I'll get it."

"Sit and relax. I'm on my way."

She watched as he walked away, his boots making a rhythmic thump on the cement floor. Out of the corner of her eye, she could see her bunkmates watching, too.

Jesse returned and set down a steaming mug in front of her. Nothing like the smell of coffee.

Nothing like a sexy bull rider!

"Thanks."

"Sorry, the cookies were gone. Nothing but crumbs left."

He sat down opposite her and took a long draw on his coffee. "Good stuff, but a little weak. Coffee has to be strong enough to float a horseshoe in it."

Sara took a sip, and tried not to choke. "I could take the rust off my car with this stuff." They both laughed and that seemed to clear the air. Then Jesse crossed his arms.

Here comes the lecture.

"Sara, if you recall, there were a lot of questions on the Camp Care application form that weren't just yes, or no. If I remember Mickey's correctly, and I'm sure I do, there was a question that asked, 'What do you hope that Camp Care would do to help the applicant?' You replied that Mickey needs a break from you, needs a good male role model and that you need to refill your well. Right?"

"Something like that, but where is this conversation going?"

"Do you think I am a good role model?" he asked.

She remembered the Cowboy Code discussion and how the wranglers were hanging on to his every word. He scored with the red bandannas and the burping contest, and without a doubt he read each wrangler's folder from cover to cover and was taking his job seriously.

Maybe she ought to give him a break and see what else he could do.

"Yes. I think you're a good role model, Jesse."

"And let me point out that it's going to be harder for you to get a break from Mickey and vice versa because you're here."

She shrugged. "That's obvious, but I seem to be missing your point."

"If you think Mickey needs a break from you, and you need to refill your well, relax a bit!"

She spoke through gritted teeth. "What did you say?"

"Stop smothering your son. If you want your other goals to be met, don't take away Mickey's candy. Don't make him wear a jacket. Don't listen in on our discussions. Don't even congratulate him on winning the burping contest. Pretend he's not here."

Sara stood up so quickly her chair fell over and made a banging noise that echoed throughout the empty hall.

"Is there anything else you need to add, Mr. Beaumont, before I make an appointment to speak with Lori Floyd in the morning to get Mickey removed from your bunkhouse?"

"I think I covered it all." He pushed his hat back with a thumb. "Sara, what happened to our truce?"

"I think you broke our truce when you trashed me."

"When you talked about taking Mickey's candy away and making sure he was wearing a jacket, well, it bothered me. You're not letting him be a boy, and you're pulling him away from kids his age. Kids he is bonding with. I'm just surprised you didn't threaten to move him from Bunkhouse 13 before, due to the burping contest."

"I'd thought about it."

Deep inside, she knew that he was right. She had to back off and give Mickey some space. She picked up the chair and sat back down.

Yes. He was right. He was as smart as he was sexy.

"Tomorrow the equine therapy program starts. I'll be teaching Bunkhouse 13 how to ride. Think you can handle it?"

"My son on a horse?"

"Yes, ma'am."

Her stomach turned. "I won't be able to handle it."

"Mickey will love it. Trust me."

"Trust?" She flashed back to her late husband telling her to trust him. That he wasn't going to drink anymore. That he wasn't going to stop for a drink and come right home from work.

"This is going to be tough. I'm going to have to watch him," she said.

"I don't think so. Let him be. Or I'll carry you away over my shoulder."

"How dare you!"

"Oh, you haven't seen anything yet, Sara. Trust me."

Chapter 5

Jesse had been looking forward to this morning all week. This was the day that he introduced his wranglers to taking care of their assigned horses. Later, Jesse and a certified equine therapy instructor would work together.

He wanted to learn as much as he could, too.

Jesse walked to the shower shed, which contained special showers and bathrooms shared between two bunkhouses. Each one had state-of-the-art equipment for various impairments along with huge dressing rooms. Those who couldn't bathe themselves had help.

As Jesse shaved, he thought about how he never tired of watching the excited, yet wary, faces of new riders when they got on a horse. He would teach them how to brush, feed and to be comfortable with their assigned animal. The wranglers wouldn't be required to saddle or bridle their mounts, but Jesse would teach them how to clean the tack and put it away.

The first time they mounted and sat upright in their appropriate saddles, they always looked like they were sitting on top of the world.

And when the horse moved...there was excitement and white-knuckle fright. It was his job to get the wranglers to relax and enjoy the experience.

He had a copy of the lesson plans and he and four other ramrods were going to take the lead on rolling out the equine therapy program. Jesse, because he had the least experience working with children, was assigned to Group A, the kids without physical limitations.

Mickey Peterson was in his group of five on Monday, Wednesday and Friday. Jesse tried each of the horses and picked out Socks for Mickey. J.B. McIntosh would ride Banner, and Glen Stoney would have Snowball. Ty would ride Blondie.

Socks was a jet-black mare with four white socks and a white patch above her nose. Sara Peterson would be thrilled to know that Socks had been evaluated on numerous occasions and all reports indicated that she was gentle and good with kids.

Yes, Sara would be happy, and she'd be happier to learn that Mickey would walk Socks around the corral numerous times by a lead rope with a volunteer before Mickey would ever ride by himself. Jesse felt strongly that new riders should be comfortable with their horse before they ever put a shoe inside the stirrup.

He jumped in the shower. He liked these early times when none of his young charges were stirring, but it soon would be loud chaos, even though four out of the eight kids didn't speak.

Not yet anyway.

As the hot water rained down on him, he vowed to help each and every wrangler in his care. He didn't mind if he had to sit with the professional staff every free moment that he had in addition to the regular scheduled meetings; he was going to do everything possible.

Those whose mobility was impaired—Steve, Brendon, Jackson and David—he wanted to make stronger. They'd ride on Tuesdays and Thursdays with extra staff to assist them. Riding would strengthen their core and they might use different muscles. Their horses would be their legs.

Jesse began to hear his wranglers talking and moving around, so he hurriedly toweled himself off and slipped into his underwear, a pair of well-worn jeans and a long-sleeved chambray shirt. After reaching for his socks, he pulled them on, followed by his work boots.

Then Jesse opened the door to the bunkhouse.

"Good morning, wranglers! As you all know, today is the day you are going to begin to learn to ride. So hit the showers and get dressed in your cowboy duds. Get a move on. You're burning daylight."

There were shouts of glee and pure turmoil as the

boys scrambled for their clothes, crutches and wheel-chairs, and hurried to the showers.

Jesse always found it entertaining.

"Don't forget to make up your bunks after your showers and before we line up for the flag raising and breakfast!" he yelled over the commotion. "Help your partner if you can. If not, give a yell for me."

When they had all departed for the shower shed, Jesse made his own bed and tidied up his area in the front of the bunkhouse. He might as well set a good example for the young cowboys.

Jesse thought about seeing Sara at breakfast. She knew that today was riding day, so she probably hadn't slept much last night. He considered their conversation last night and how she might feel about his assertion that she was smothering Mickey.

She'd probably accept it better if advice came from one of the psychiatric staff rather than a bull rider, but he called it like he saw it. Besides, he had some firsthand knowledge of Mickey, and he was a neutral party.

No, he wasn't neutral. He cared about Mickey. He cared about all his young wranglers.

His wranglers were dribbling in from the shower, making their beds and putting on their socks and boots. Then they lined up in front of the door, join-ing wranglers on foot, in wheelchairs, on crutches and motorized scooters.

When they were all lined up, and the bunkhouse was tidy, Jesse led them all to the flag circle. They were the third bunkhouse to arrive.

Jesse looked around to see if Sara was attending the ceremony, but she wasn't there. No doubt, she was busy getting breakfast ready for the wranglers and other staff, who would descend on the chuck wagon after the Pledge of Allegiance and a short nondenominational prayer.

After the flag raising, it was time for Lori to call the bunkhouse numbers for breakfast. Cabins were inspected and were ranked from cleanest to "needing help." Bunkhouse 13 was third.

As he was going through the breakfast line, he saw Sara dishing out pancakes and sausage links. Just as he thought, she looked like she hadn't slept. Her eyes were droopy and her smile was thin.

"Good morning, Sara! Great day at Camp Care, right?" Jesse asked.

"Great day," she replied, barely looking up at him. "Today's horseback riding."

"Sure is, and Mickey is one excited wrangler. I can't wait to see his face when he's sitting on his first horse."

"That's nice," she said, putting three pancakes on his plate.

"You're worried."

"Of course. That's my middle name," Sara said. She put three links of sausage next to the pancakes.

"Don't be. I've got this one."

"Please take care of him, Jesse."

"Of course. Just like I'll watch over all the kids in my care."

"He hasn't been exposed to horses," she said. "Not at all."

"Isn't therapeutic horseback riding one of the reasons why you brought Mickey all the way from New York State to Camp Care?"

"Yes," she replied, clearly reluctant to admit it.

"Well, then, it's time to ride. Cowboy up!"

"You don't understand, Jesse. Mickey is all I have."

He paused, letting that sink in. "I sure do understand. That explains a lot."

"A lot of what?" she asked.

"You're afraid you're going to lose him."

"Of course! Isn't every parent afraid of losing a child?"

"You could lose him in a lot of different ways." He shrugged. "By not letting him grow and experience things on his own you might lose him anyway. How are you helping him adjust in the real world if you overprotect him? What'll happen when he goes to college? He might flip out. Of course, that depends on whether or not you'll let him go away to school."

Sara didn't have time to answer due to the whistles and shouts for Jesse to move on down the line. There were a lot of hungry campers waiting to eat.

"Gotta get going," Jesse said. "I just wish you'd trust me to take care of Mickey."

"I don't trust anyone to take care of my son but me." She put pancakes and sausage on the next person's plate a little too absentmindedly and one of the sausages rolled onto the floor. Disappointment was visible on the boy's face, so she heaped more sausages and another pancake on his plate before he followed Jesse down the food line.

"Trust. Work on it, Sara."

Sheesh! She opened her mouth, seemingly to say something, probably because she didn't want him to have the last word, but Jesse left the line and took a seat with the rest of his wranglers, who began to ask him all kinds of questions about their riding lessons. Where he sat, he had a perfect view of Sara, who was smiling and talking to everyone who came through.

Everyone but him.

"Good morning!" Sara said cheerfully to everyone who slid their trays in front of her. The only time she seemed worried and anxious was when he passed through.

Jesse shook his head. They couldn't even talk without some sort of fight. He seemed to agitate her, and that wasn't his intent.

He intended to get to know her better as a woman, as a date, as a friend, maybe even more. He'd like nothing better than to loosen that tight bun at the nape of her neck and fluff up her blond hair. He'd cup her head in his hands, lean down, and capture her lips in his.

Then he'd brace himself for the slap that was sure to follow.

Maybe not.

Maybe it would be better if Mickey was transferred to another cabin.

No. Mickey was making good friends here in Bunkhouse 13, and it wouldn't be fair to the boy.

He'd just have to keep talking to Sara, and get her to calm down where Mickey was concerned.

Jesse had to convince her to let Mickey grow and advance. If nothing else, the boy's riding lessons should prove to Sara that Jesse was good for Mickey and the other wranglers.

And maybe, just maybe, she'd find out that there was more to him than just being a bull rider.

Sara had a little over an hour before she had to get back to the chuck wagon to help prepare lunch. It should be an easy meal. Cookie was planning on chicken soup and chicken patties on a hamburger roll with chef salad served family-style at the tables.

In the meantime, what harm would there be if she went to the corral and watched Mickey's riding lesson?

Maybe she'd just stay in the shadows and observe, instead of being front and center spying on her son.

And even if Mickey didn't think she was spying on him, Jesse Beaumont would know she was.

She kept telling herself that she wasn't worried that Mickey was going to get hurt and that she just wanted to see the happiness on his face that Jesse was sure he'd feel when he got up on a horse for the first time.

Sara hurried for the copse of trees that looked like they might be pines and some kind of bushes bunched on the left side of the corral's mammoth doors. If she positioned herself correctly in the vegetation, she'd be able to see the action.

She looked around to see if anyone noticed her. So far, so good. Slanting herself to move through the bushes, she dodged the sharp needles of the trees, wishing she had a long-sleeved blouse on instead of her neon-yellow Camp Care T-shirt.

She moved the branches away to get closer to see. That was a mistake, as sap clung to her hands, then a branch got stuck in her hair. Slowly, she pulled her hair from the sticky pine needles and worked on removing a pine cone from behind her ear.

There wasn't much action in the corral, just a couple of cowboy types chewing on blades of hay and talking. The kids apparently were still being taught some basics in the barn instead of on horseback, thank goodness.

Hoping that Mickey's lesson might get rained out, she looked up at the sky. Unfortunately, it was a bright blue without clouds. The sun and a slight breeze made it a perfect day for a horseback ride.

What kind of a mother was she to hope that it would rain on Mickey's riding day?

Selfish. She was just absolutely selfish.

Was it being selfish to hope that her son didn't get hurt? To want him to stay away from activities that might hurt him?

Jesse had a point. Equine therapy was one of the reasons why she'd chosen Camp Care for Mickey, why it had come highly recommended by her therapist, by Mickey's counselors and his psychologist, all of whom had firsthand knowledge of Camp Care success stories.

Her heart began thumping in her chest when she recognized J.B., one of Mickey's bunkhouse friends, on a chestnut horse, being led by one of the ramrods.

She could see Glen grinning from ear to ear under the helmet that he wore, sitting on top of the world.

He didn't say a word, but a big, sudden laugh came from deep inside him. Even Glen looked stunned at the raspy sound he emitted.

The ramrod laughed, too. "Yeehaw! Ride 'em, cowboy!"

Sara would love to hear a laugh from Mickey. It had been a long time.

Looking equally thrilled, another rider and ramrod came out of the barn and followed J.B. in walking around the corral.

The two horses passed in front of her, and she could hear the breathing of both horse and rider and the squeaking of the leather saddle.

Sara held her breath. Mickey had to be next! She moved another branch to get a better view.

His head was bent, and she couldn't tell whether or not Mickey was smiling underneath his helmet.

"Mickey, keep your head up so you can see where you're going," she heard Jesse say.

Mickey definitely was smiling. Sara let out her breath, watching him closely for any sign of duress on her son's face, and making sure that Jesse was calm and cool.

"You're doing great, Mickey. Keep your legs straight. This is really cool, isn't it, cowboy? By the end of the week, you'll be riding alone around the corral, riding without being led."

Riding without being led!

Another thing for Sara to worry about down the line.

But as Mickey and Jesse passed by her, Mickey's smile couldn't be any wider. She even thought she'd heard him make a sound of excitement.

Mickey hadn't shown enthusiasm since before the accident.

Jesse looked her way and tweaked his hat. "I'll bet your mother wishes she was here to see you ride. She'd see how much fun you were having and how you look like you're the King of the Cowboys. Wouldn't she be surprised to see how safe you are, too?"

He knows I'm here!

It must be her bright yellow shirt that had given her away.

Her face heated. Her first thought was to flee, but she still wanted to watch Mickey, so she stayed in the brush, hiding like an international spy, dodging pine cones and sap.

And a spider!

Not a spider. Anything but a spider!

The thing was small, but it hovered on a thin strand of web right in front of her nose.

Sara stifled a scream. She didn't know anything about Oklahoma spiders; she was used to the ones in New York. New York spiders were hideous, but she didn't know of any whose bite would kill her.

But this little black thing…well, it might as well be a tarantula.

The scream was still in her throat, choking her, ready to erupt.

Do something!

Mickey rode by, sitting straighter in the saddle, and looking more confident.

Cross-eyed, she kept one eye on Mickey, and the other on the spider dangling in front of her face on a thin strand.

She didn't know how much longer she'd be able to hold out. She had to do something—*anything!*—before Mickey's next circle around the corral.

Slowly, Sara moved her hand to an area above the strand and was able to bring the spider down to the ground.

At least that's what she thought she was doing. She moved her hand to wipe the hair out of her face, and the spider came along with her hand.

It was now on her face. She could feel it crawling.

Okay. She was going to let out the granddaddy of all screams. She had every right to, but she neither wanted to spook the horses in the corral nor did she want to call attention to herself, so she shook her head and wiped her face, ran her hands down her clothes and hopped in place. Maybe Mr. Spider was finally gone now.

Jesse and Mickey walked by her. Jesse tweaked his hat again at her. "This is our last trip, Mickey, and we're going to go back into the barn where I'll teach you how to clean the tack. So, if anyone is watching, it'd be a good time for him or her to go about their day."

Jesse stopped in front of her hideout. "Mickey, did you enjoy your ride?"

The boy nodded as if his head was loose from his neck. Then he slapped Jesse's hand in a high five.

Sara's heart was about to burst. A high five! It might not be much, but it was like climbing Mount Everest for Mickey.

Yes. Mickey had a wonderful time, he was safe and she had Jesse to thank.

She'd see them both for lunch soon, and she'd give anything if Mickey would talk and tell her about his riding.

Until then, she'd better get cleaned up and see what she could find to get the pine sap off.

Then she'd hurry to the chuck wagon.

Before she took the final step out of the bushes, she looked around to make sure no one would be around to witness her exit.

All clear.

As she hurried to her bunkhouse, she thought about how Jesse was going to tease her for lurking so she could spy on Mickey's lesson.

"Smothering" was going to be in his first sentence, or at least his second.

Chapter 6

As Jesse helped the wranglers clean the tack and put it away under the watchful eyes of the equine therapist, he chuckled to himself.

Sara had been hiding in the bushes. He saw the yellow shirt, could smell her special scent as he passed by leading Mickey's horse. Lilacs, he guessed, although he didn't know one flower from another.

At one point, he thought she was going to bust out of the bushes during the lesson. Something was wrong. He wasn't worried; the horses were trained so thoroughly they wouldn't react if they were startled, but he'd have to ask her what had happened.

He wanted to tell her that now she could relax, but it wouldn't do any good. The program would keep progressing until some of the wranglers were able to ride without being led. The ramrods and equine therapists would still be with the wranglers at all times, but there needed to be more of a challenge for the kids.

They all wanted to be "cowboys."

He sent his charges off to lunch, and Jesse washed his hands, tossed some water on his face, then combed his hair. After drying his face and hands with his bandanna, he then stuffed it back into his back pocket and proceeded up the path to the chuck wagon.

He was looking forward to seeing Sara and wondered if she'd mention her foray into the foliage.

Foray into the foliage?

Since when had he gotten so poetic?

Maybe it was because Sara intrigued him. He'd never met anyone like her. She aggravated him and frustrated him, but when he saw her doing yoga, she was calm and still—that is, up until the time they opened their mouths and they fought.

Opening the door to the chuck wagon, he went inside. The noise was deafening. The first thing he did was to look toward the metal tables, steaming from hot water underneath the big pans to keep the food hot, where Sara worked.

She met his gaze, but quickly looked away.

Was she watching for him?

Hmm…that made him walk a little taller as he headed for the chow line.

"Hi, Sara. How's your day going? Did you do anything special?"

She shrugged. "Nothing special. It was just a usual day. How about you?"

Sara set two chicken sandwiches on his plate.

"I took my class around the corral. Mickey did a great job and really loved it. Too bad you weren't able to see him."

"Um...uh-huh." She kept her head down, and Jesse bent at the waist to peek under the glass shield, hoping to see her face.

He laughed at her response, then stood and laughed more. Once he started, he couldn't stop.

Sara joined in. She laughed so hard, she started gasping for breath.

Soon everyone in the chuck wagon was laughing along with them. Anyone who walked through the door looked surprised, then they joined in.

Jesse stepped around the steam table, took Sara's hand, and led her into a corner of the chuck wagon, out of sight of the eyes of the diners.

"Sara?" He tightened his arms around her, pulled her near him. Yes, lilacs.

The merriment in her eyes faded, replaced by panic. She stiffened. "Jesse, I—I...it's been such a long time. You have no idea."

He bent his head again, but Sara pushed his arms. "It's not the right time, Jesse. I'm sorry."

Jesse didn't know what he was thinking. All he knew was that he wanted to kiss Sara when they were both in a happy, playful mood. He wanted to crush her body to his, and kiss her perfect lips—lips that were turned up into a smile.

"We'll talk. Okay?" he said.

She touched her hairnet, and that seemed to bring her back to reality. "I have to get back to my station. The laughter has stopped."

It might have for now but he was going to bring laughter back to Sara.

She needed to just give him time.

Sara had wanted to kiss Jesse, desperately. The atmosphere was light and fun and when he pulled her into the corner by the supply shelves, she knew exactly what he wanted.

But she'd pulled away.

Jesse was a player; she was a widow and before that was in a platonic marriage. A marriage that had been just hanging on for Mickey. Any love that she might have had for her husband had faded a little more with every drink he took. Mike was the only man she really knew, the only man she'd ever kissed.

There were a few stragglers coming in for lunch, and Sara greeted them and passed out sandwiches. Turning to Julia who was ladling out chicken soup, she asked, "Jules, can you cover my station? I'm going to get a little time off before dinner prep starts."

"Of course. Go!" Cookie waved her away, and Sara hurried to her bunkhouse.

Luckily, the cabin was empty, so she didn't have to be cordial. She put on shorts and a tank top, stepped into a pair of flip-flops, and hurried to the lake with a towel under her arm.

She needed to do yoga to clear her mind.

Maybe then she could figure out why on earth she didn't stay in Jesse's arms earlier and kiss him until her knees buckled.

Perhaps it was because she barely knew him—she wasn't sure she even completely liked him—and because it had just been a wild time in the chuck wagon, with everyone laughing.

It would have been crazy to kiss him. They were at a kids' camp, for heaven's sake! Stealing kisses by the metal storage shelves? Soon they'd be skinny-dipping in the lake!

Her face heated just thinking about that, then the warmth spread through her body. Maybe she should take a dip in the lake first.

Sara couldn't remember the last time she'd done something on the spur of the moment, but she did so now; she sprinted the rest of the way, ran into the shallow part of the lake and then dived in.

Cold! She just remembered that Jesse had told her that it was a spring-fed lake. Where did the springs come from? A glacier behind the trees?

She swam around a bit to keep moving, then walked to the patch of grass. Shivering, she wrapped the towel around her. Turning her face up to the afternoon sun, she'd dry off in no time.

That was fun! She smiled, trying to remember when she'd done something that spontaneous. She was like a kid at camp herself!

Standing, she was just about to start her yoga program with Salute the Sun, when she heard someone walking on the small stones along the lakeside. She sat back down.

"Do you want to talk?"

It was Jesse. Her heart skipped a beat or ten. His smile, those perfect white teeth. He sported a pair of warm-up pants, navy blue with an orange stripe down the outside of each leg, that hung casually, barely clinging to his hips.

Sara's smile faded. She knew he'd want to rehash what had happened. She didn't want to, but maybe she owed him an explanation.

"I was going to do yoga," she said, buying herself some time.

"Do you mind if I do it with you?"

"Not at all. It's another perfect day to do yoga by the lake. I was just going to start."

"I hate to burst your bubble, but swimming lessons start tomorrow. This lake will rock and roll with the kids splashing enough to start a tsunami."

"I can hardly wait." She shaded her eyes to look up at him. "I guess I'll have to find another secret spot."

"Secret from me, too?"

Sara grinned. "I'll have to keep it a secret from you the most."

He clutched at his heart. "I'm hurt."

"Don't be."

She liked bantering with Jesse. He kept her on her toes.

Oh, but she hoped he didn't think she was flirting with him. She'd never had a knack for that.

"Let's do it," Jesse said.

"Huh?" She wasn't going to bite.

Jesse unbuttoned his shirt. It was nothing, really, but it was one of the sexiest things she'd seen in ages. The cowboy had a muscular body that rippled in all the right places. His biceps were huge. Even if she hadn't seen him doing push-ups yesterday, she could tell that he worked out regularly.

Sara ran through her usual routine: Salute the Sun, Cat, Chair, Cobra, Bridge, and then she launched into the more difficult poses.

Jesse followed her perfectly.

When she was done, she turned to him and bowed. "Namaste, Jesse."

"Namaste."

"After my yoga, I usually meditate, but I think you came out here to talk. Right, Jesse?"

"Right as rain."

"So, go ahead and talk. I figure that you want to talk about our non-kiss." She dreaded talking about it, but she might as well get the awkwardness out of the way.

"Let's start with you hiding in the bushes."

"Must we?"

"We must." Jesse grabbed his shirt that was hanging over one of the larger rocks and shrugged into it.

"So, why the bushes? Why didn't you just lean over the corral post?" he asked.

"I didn't want my son, and you, to think that I was spying on him."

"But you were."

"But he doesn't have to know that." Sara winced. "You don't think that Mickey saw me, do you?"

"I'll guarantee you that he was so busy concentrating on riding that nothing else existed. Did you see how much he loved it? Mickey even shot J.B. a dirty look because J.B. made a snorting noise when I talked about geldings and how they got that way."

"That's my son. He loves to learn. He's an A student." Sara sat up straighter. "But Mickey's still way too serious."

"There's more," Jesse said.

"I'm listening."

"Mickey cleaned the tack like a demon, and he held out his hand for me to shake when I dismissed everyone for lunch."

"No!" She gasped. "Mickey doesn't really react or interact much. Not since the accident anyway."

"Maybe he's starting to come out of his shell. Okay? Let me handle it."

She raised an eyebrow. "Let you handle it? Handle what?"

"I want to bring him out more. Mickey needs socialization more than the rest of my guys. The burping contest was a big score. His first day on horseback was another big score. I don't want you hovering over him."

"I suppose that your animal husbandry classes in community college taught you how to help a boy socialize, right?"

Jesse shook his head. "Let's not start this again. I know I don't have the academic credentials, but I've been out there in the world. And the camp therapists agree with my action plans for each kid. With their evaluations and conclusions and mine, it'll all merge together, and we'll help the kids."

She didn't say anything…yet.

He sighed. "Look, Sara. Let's forget it. Maybe we should have begun with talking about my attempted kiss, but I think that right now, I just don't feel like it." He turned to leave.

She didn't want him to leave in a negative mood because of her.

"Jesse, it was funny—everyone laughing in the chuck wagon. It was just plain funny."

"Yeah, it was. And only you and I know that the joke was on you."

"I know." She grinned. "And I'll leave Mickey alone. I can see that he's safe with you watching over him. All the kids are safe."

He turned to go again, then looked over his shoulder. "Just one more thing—what was all that rustling you did in the bushes?"

"There was a spider. I hate them. The thing was all over me, and I didn't want to scream or burst out of the bushes and upset the horses. That would have given me away."

"Yeah, it would have. And you would have embarrassed Mickey, too. It's gotta be tough for him to have his mother here."

"I…um…never thought of that." She tried to place herself in Mickey's cowboy boots. Yes, she'd be mortified if her mother had come to camp with her. Camp was for letting loose a little, being independent, making new friends and having new experiences.

And she was clinging to Mickey like a piece of lint!

But she had to stick up for herself. "I just had to see him ride, Jesse. I had to see his face. There was no harm done. He didn't see me."

"I know, Sara. You *are* here with him, and watching him ride would be hard for anyone to pass up. In this instance, I'd do the same thing."

"Oh! You—you!" She wished she had something to throw at him for putting her through feelings of regret—of being a smotherer, and an overprotective mother.

Sara stood and walked to her bunkhouse, thinking about what Jesse had said. She might as well change out of her freezing wet clothes and get to the chuck wagon early for dinner, to make up time.

Even though they'd be just passing through her station, Sara was looking forward to asking Mickey about how his riding went and watching his face for signs of happiness. Also, she had to admit that she couldn't wait to see Jesse again.

But why? She'd had enough of his parenting lectures.

It was the almost kiss. Oh, how she wanted to kiss him, but something was holding her back. She'd heard that Jesse was a player and had been around his share of buckle bunnies; maybe she didn't want to be another one. Or maybe she didn't want to be compared to his other women.

Where's your confidence, huh, Sara?

As the years went by, her late husband had made her feel unwanted as a woman; she was just a fixture, like a lamp or an end table.

She didn't really love him, either. She liked him. He was okay, a good provider and fine with Mickey. That's why she stayed with him.

She was rusty and scared to get involved with Jesse.

Swinging open the door to her bunkhouse, she entered. There, a small group of her bunkmates huddled together.

"We were just talking about you," said Jules.

"Oh?"

Jules sighed. "Yeah, we all saw you and Jesse Beaumont hugging in the corner, and were wondering if you two are an item? Is there any hope for any of us with him?"

"There's lots of hope for all of you." Sara laughed. "We aren't an item."

Surprisingly, it bothered her to say that.

Patty giggled. "He's just gorgeous, and he's interested in you. What are you waiting for?"

"It's a long story, and my love life is nonexistent, and my son takes up all my time…well…" She shrugged, shocked at how much she'd just told relative strangers about her life.

Jules raised an index finger in the air. "What you need, Sara, is a summer fling! Jesse will be at the party tonight for the ramrods and staff. Time for some romantic dancing."

A summer fling?

No way!

Then again, why not?

The next time Jesse Beaumont wanted to kiss her, she was going to kiss him back…and more.

Jesse had another beginners' class, the other half of Bunkhouse 13, to teach at the barn and corral. He was looking forward to it. It would probably be a quiet one, with no one lurking in the bushes.

He was still chuckling over that one.

He was still stumped over Sara's reaction to his almost kiss. Adrenaline shot through him, and he wanted to share more time with Sara.

But she had other ideas.

Sara continued to be a mystery to him, but he was going to break down the emotional walls surrounding her, block by concrete block.

He assumed that Sara would be at the party tonight. He should have asked her to be his date, was up for some boot scootin' and to cut loose. It'd been ages since he'd been with his fellow bull riders at a honky-tonk taking over the dance floor and the bar, and being around all the single women.

But before he could think about the dance, he had to think about the next equine group.

The other half of his wranglers from Bunkhouse 13 needed more attention due to their physical challenges. There was still one ramrod to one wrangler on a horse with an equine therapist and another four ramrods standing by.

Everything went perfectly; the wranglers had a great time, and they soaked up all of his information like a sponge.

After tack cleaning, they put everything away. Then Jesse dismissed the class for dinner.

As he washed up, he thought about how he wanted to show Sara a good time tonight at the dance. He suspected that she hadn't been out in a while. He should have asked her personally, but he just assumed that the entire staff would be there to cut loose from their charges. The wranglers were having game night tonight, supervised by the roving ramrods.

Sometime during the evening he wanted to have a good conversation with Sara so he could learn more about her.

What was wrong with him? Were his buckle bunny days a thing of the past? After all, his brothers had settled down, and they had been worse than him.

Jesse never lacked for female companionship or a woman willing to warm his bed. He was even getting interested looks from the female staff, but Sara Peterson was keeping him at a distance.

But he was up for the challenge.

Chapter 7

Sara didn't have much time on the dinner line except to ask Mickey how his ride went and to spoon a Sloppy Joe on his plate before he moved on.

She was rewarded by a big grin from her son.

When Jesse came through, he smiled and told her that he'd see her at the dance that night.

Jules elbowed her in the side at that remark, and Sara hoped that Jesse didn't read anything into that. She wouldn't want him to think that she was chasing him.

Not now anyway.

The words *summer fling* kept rolling through her mind. She couldn't think of anyone else who was more of a good time guy than Jesse; Sara had had a lot of time being a mother, and now she needed to feel like a woman, if only for a while.

Unfortunately, there was a lot of cleanup after the meal, which cut into her preparation for the party. She had hoped that her bunkmates would help her with makeup and find her something suitable to wear out of the clothes that she'd brought.

"I haven't been to a party in ages," she told them later in the bunkhouse. "Actually, I haven't gone anywhere in ages."

The invitations stopped coming after Michael died. It seemed as though no one in their circle of friends wanted an extra person. She wouldn't have accepted their invitations, anyway, because she'd never hire a babysitter for Mickey.

She was going to launch her plan tonight. A shock of excitement ran through her as she thought about dancing with Jesse. She'd work up the courage to ask him to dance—a slow dance.

Sara felt like a giddy teenager. She and her bunkmates all shared makeup, passed around clothes and jewelry, and laughed.

When the dust settled, she wore a pastel sundress, a white bolero sweater scattered with sequins and white strappy sandals.

She looked in the half mirror at the back end of the bunkhouse and barely recognized herself. Her bun was gone and her hair, let down around her shoulders, shone; her green eyes twinkled in merriment, and they really popped with a smoky lavender eye shadow.

If only she knew how to flirt. No. She was too old for that. She was just going to be herself, but lighter, less intense, and maybe they could avoid talking about her parenting.

They all walked to the recreation center, laughing and joking as they went. The moon shone above, the weather was perfect and she could hear the music coming from the center.

She wondered if Jesse was there yet. She'd soon know.

As she walked in, she saw Jesse at the edge of what was the dance floor. He sure looked fabulous. He sported a pair of jeans that he was born to wear, shiny boots and a blue-and-red-checked shirt, and a belt buckle that was the size of Oklahoma, topped off by a white cowboy hat. He was surrounded by a group of four women that Sara recognized as being from the therapy staff.

She followed her bunkmates to a table, and she sat where she could secretly watch Jesse.

Garth Brooks was singing about friends in low places, a fun song. During the chorus, everyone chimed in, including Sara.

More people came to Jesse's circle, mostly women, while Sara sat on her butt.

He was so busy talking and entertaining all the women around him, he didn't seem to even know she was there.

Why should he? He wasn't looking for her. But Sara couldn't take her eyes off Jesse.

As more music played, she watched him. Everyone was hanging on his every word, and when he threw his head back and laughed, everyone laughed with him.

A slow, sweet song by Alison Krauss played, and she knew that this was the one she wanted to dance to with Jesse. She called on every gut she had, got up and walked across the dance floor.

She met Jesse's gaze, and she could hear him excuse himself from his group. Walking toward her, he held out his arms, and she walked into them.

"I thought you'd never ask," Sara said, inhaling his scents of cedar and leather.

"I noticed you looking at me."

She smiled. "You must be mistaken."

"I must be. So?" he asked. "How do I look?"

"Are you fishing for compliments?"

"Hell, yes!"

Sara could feel the warmth of his hand through her cotton dress. "You look like a cowboy."

"And you look…um…beautiful. Very beautiful."

Her first inclination was to tell him that he had the wrong person. She wasn't beautiful at all.

But tonight she felt like it.

"Thanks, Jesse. That's nice of you to say."

He pulled her tighter to his body, and her knees grew weak. She couldn't remember the last time she was dancing in a man's arms. Yes, she could. It was her wedding.

She loved dancing; Michael didn't. The few weddings they were invited to, Michael drank and Sara sat at the table, watching everyone else dance.

She didn't want to think of Michael, though; she wanted to experience Jesse Beaumont.

He was a masterful dancer, but she kept up with him. When the song was over, he didn't move to release her, but moved a couple inches back.

"That was nice, Sara."

"You're a wonderful dancer. You're easy to follow."

"That wasn't what I meant."

Before she could ask him what he meant, they were interrupted.

"How about a dance, cowboy?" the woman asked. Sara didn't recognize her, but guessed she was with the office staff.

"I'm dancing with Sara, here. How about a rain check for later, Brittney?"

"You got it, Jesse. I'll be back. I want to talk to you about bull riding." Brittney turned and strode away.

Sara smiled. "She's very pretty, and she knows about bull riding?"

"Yeah. She's a fan."

"I don't know anything about it."

Jesse nodded. "I think that when it starts up again at the end of August, you should come to an event."

"I'll be back in New York then. The bull riding never goes there, does it?"

"In January, for the last several years, we've been going to Madison Square Garden. Talk about iconic!"

"Sure is. I had no idea." She thought about that. "Hey, you're a jock!"

He chuckled. "I guess you could say that." He held out his hands. "Another dance?"

"I think I'm monopolizing you. There are ladies stacked up like cordwood waiting to dance with you."

Jesse stepped closer to Sara and gathered her into his arms. "I guess I like being monopolized."

She could feel his strong biceps through his shirt. She remembered how he did push-ups without a shirt on. He worked at his sport. That didn't surprise her, because he was high in the PBR standings with his two brothers. That she knew from her bunkmates.

He whispered to her. "I don't even know what you do in Henderson Falls."

"I used to be the business manager and accountant for a small appliance store, and once in a while I'd sell something for a commission, but I was laid off when the boss's son took over."

"Then when you go back home—"

"I'll have to land a job, and fast."

But Sara didn't want to talk about herself. She wanted to talk about him.

"Jesse, you'll have to tell me how bull riding works." She decided that she wanted to learn, wanted to understand more about his world. It was a genuine request; she wasn't just flirting.

"Fifty points for the rider, fifty points for the bull. Stay on for eight seconds using only one arm, and don't touch the bull. Try not to get stomped on when you get off. Highest score wins."

"Um…sounds easy," she said sarcastically.

"It's not."

"I was just kidding."

"I know."

For the rest of the dance, she rested her cheek on his shoulder and felt his hands on her back, felt the light scratch of his jeans on the skirt of her sundress and inhaled his scent.

At one particularly brave moment, she gently rubbed the back of his neck because she wanted to feel the softness of his hair.

Sara could feel the vibration that started deep in Jesse's chest and ended in a moan of pleasure.

She raised an eyebrow. Did she do that?

She wasn't a seductress in the least. It'd been a long time since she'd had the opportunity to touch a man.

Jesse had her hormones going all haywire, and it proved to her that she did need a fling.

Jesse was a player. He'd be willing.

Her heart pounded wildly in her chest. She was sure that he could feel it, he was so close to her, too close.

The music ended, but they were still swaying. Looking up at Jesse, she whispered, "Thanks for the dance. I—I—It's been a long time since I've danced like this."

He shook his head. "That's something I hope to rectify."

A country line dance came on, and everyone scurried for a place on the dance floor. "I'll just watch," she said.

"Oh, no, you don't!" Jesse took her hand and they got a place in line, second row.

"Jesse! Jesse Beaumont, you have to lead us!" came a voice from the crowd. "Jesse can really line dance."

Her bunkmates Kelli and Jules each took one of his arms and led him to the front of the line dancers.

"Okay! Let's boot scoot!" Jesse shouted.

An Alan Jackson song was playing, with a perfect beat for dancing. Sara had a perfect view of Jesse's backside as he led the dancers. They were right. He really could scoot his boots.

Sara followed Jesse the best she could, but mostly tried not to bump into the people around her. She laughed and had a great time. By the end of the song, she was keeping up when she wasn't distracted by Jesse's butt.

Another fast song came on, but Sara found a path through the crowd and made it back to her seat. She wanted to sit for a while and think.

Jesse made it through another dance before he joined her at the table.

He wiped his face with a black bandanna. "Would you like to join me outside for some fresh air?"

"Absolutely."

He held out his hand for Sara to take.

Sara knew that if she took his hand and left with

Jesse, they'd be considered a couple by the staff of Camp Care.

She still took his hand, and they made their way outside.

Jesse looked up at the sky. "There's a full moon. I think we can find our way to the lake."

Her heart beat wildly and butterflies danced in her stomach. Going off alone with Jesse to their spot by the lake was dangerous.

All nerves aside, she wanted to go, wanted to be with him.

"We can find our way. I have a cell phone with a flashlight on it. It's not good for reception anywhere in Camp Care, but I keep it in hand for a flashlight."

"Now, that's a good camper."

Jesse's hand was still closed around hers as he led the way.

Instead of their usual patch of grass, which was wet, they sat on some large rocks.

"People are talking about us, Jesse."

He chuckled. "Let them, but tell me, Sara, what's going on?"

Her stomach lurched. "What do you mean?"

"I mean, what were you doing to my neck?" He raised an eyebrow.

Telling him that she wanted to feel the softness of his hair seemed so juvenile. "What were you doing pulling me so tightly to you?"

"That's dancing. And I remember that you laid your head on my shoulder."

"That's dancing," Sara echoed.

They laughed. Then Sara remembered their dance, and a shiver went up her spine.

"You're cold," Jesse said. "I'm sorry that I didn't bring a coat because it was so nice out, and that little sweater of yours doesn't help much to warm you."

"I'm okay."

"Trust me." Jesse wrapped his arm around her shoulders, pulling her toward him. Sara felt warm immediately, hot even. "How's this?"

"It's nice, Jesse." She settled into his arms. If she were to turn her head just a little, she'd be a mere whisper from his lips.

"Just think, a while ago, we were fighting like two world champs. Now, we're all cuddled up like this," he said. "It's hard to believe. What changed, Sara?"

"Maybe it's because we weren't talking about Mickey and the fact that you think I smother him."

Jesse took her hand and played with her fingers. "Let's not talk about Mickey. He's with Bunkhouses 12 and 11. The kids are playing games with Roving Ramrod Ronnie."

"I know he's fine, Jesse, but I don't need to talk about Mickey right now."

"What? That's huge for you!"

"I know."

"So, what do you want to talk about?" he asked.

"I want to talk about our almost kiss this afternoon."

"Whenever you're ready. I'm listening."

She threaded her fingers into his. "It was a fun time with how we got everyone laughing. Something like that might never happen again, and it was exciting and fun. And when you pulled me into the corner and you were going to kiss me…well, I chickened out."

"I guess I rushed you. I just wanted to share the moment—"

"I know, Jesse, and any other woman would have been excited back. Except me. You see, it's been a long time, and I am very…uh…rusty. My marriage to Michael…well…it was comfortable."

"Sara, you don't have to tell me—"

"No. It's okay. It's just that I haven't been kissed by a man in an eternity, and then there was you, and—"

"And we are here by the lake. The moon is shining, making the water sparkle, and there's a gentle lapping of the waves. If we are quiet, we can hear it."

Sara didn't move. She was hypnotized by the water and his words.

"And what if I leaned over, and lightly put my hand on the back of your head, pulling you closer to me, and put my lips over yours and gave you a soft, gentle kiss?"

Spellbound, Sara closed the space between them and touched her lips to Jesse's. She couldn't get enough; she kissed him again and again, and he met her every move. If this was a fling with a bull rider, she didn't want it to end.

Even with her inexperience, she could tell that this cowboy had lots of practice. What he could teach her!

And Sara knew she'd never be the same again.

* * *

Jesse Beaumont had to hide his budding erection. Sara was both teasing and tormenting him with her kisses.

Tentative at first, she blossomed into a great kisser!

When the lightning flashed and the thunder rolled, it summarized his feelings nicely.

He'd started falling for Sara Peterson the first time he saw her defending her son at the assay office, and now he wanted to get to know her better and to kiss the stuffing out of her, but not necessarily in that order.

"I think we'd better get back to the party before we get drenched."

She looked toward the bunkhouse area. "I have to find Mickey. He's scared of thunder and lightning."

"Mickey will be fine, Sara. Leave him alone."

She didn't say a word, but hustled up the path.

Sheesh. She had to be careful before she blew an ankle, or worse. "Slow down, Sara. Wait for me."

"No. I have to get to Mickey."

Here we go again! Jesse thought.

It started to rain. Big, fat, cold raindrops. Then the speed picked up and black clouds covered the moon.

"Sara, stop! You're going to hurt yourself!" Tree roots and outcroppings of rocks were scattered along the path. If Sara couldn't see where she was going, she could trip and fall.

Jesse was soaked to the skin and felt a chill. Sara, in her thin dress, must be freezing.

He was finally able to reach her. He grabbed a hand, then both shoulders, and held her in place, facing him.

"Sara! Sara, what the hell are you doing?"

She looked at Jesse as if she'd never seen him before.

"Look at me, Sara. Look at me." It was as if she was possessed by some kind of demon. "Dammit, Sara, stop and think about what you're doing!"

"I—I need to get to Mickey. He'll be scared." She wiped the rain from her face.

"No. You don't need to get to Mickey. Mickey is fine, and I'll prove it to you."

"How?"

"We are going to hide in the bushes under the eaves and spy on him. You've done that before." He chuckled and squeezed her hands. "So, calm down. I'd bet a gold belt buckle that Mickey is doing fine, and you're worrying for nothing."

He added, "Mickey might be jumpy, but he can handle it until the storm passes. He's with a bunch of his peers, and if you make a scene, you're going to embarrass him. They'll tease him unmercifully."

She nodded slightly. Rain dripped off the ends of her hair and dissolved into the ground.

"Besides, it looks like you're ready for a wet T-shirt contest. Sex ed isn't in the guidelines that they gave us."

Thunder roared and lightning flared, as Sara looked down at the bodice of her dress. Her eyes grew wide. Pulling the fabric away from her body, she looked up at him.

"Thank you. Good catch," she said. "I would be really embarrassing to Mickey with my bra showing."

"Aww...hell." He reached for Sara, pulled her into a hug, brushed the wet hair from her face and whispered. "It's a perfect night for spying. Let's go."

Chapter 8

Jesse couldn't believe he was doing this. He should have discouraged Sara's behavior instead of helping her spy on her son.

And it was his dumb idea, too. She was so distraught, so crazy with wanting to get to Mickey, he had to keep her away from the kid.

He was only looking out for the boy.

He would have been mortified if his mom had visited him at camp and comforted him because of the weather.

"We'll go to Bunkhouse 12. Bunkhouses 13 and 11 are over there. We'll look in the windows."

"I can't believe we are out in this weather, but thanks for going with me, Jesse."

He shrugged. "You'd only go by yourself."

"Yeah. I would."

"No one's around in this weather, but stick to the shadows. We'll walk through 13 and go out the back to 12."

In Jesse's bunkhouse, he grabbed two towels from the stack they used for swimming and handed one to Sara. She blotted the water off her, then handed the towel back to Jesse. "Thanks."

Walking through the bunkhouse, she paused at Mickey's bunk. "Did Mickey do this?"

"Well, I didn't do it. Every wrangler takes care of their own area."

"Everything is so neat and tidy. You should see how his room at home looks." Sara rolled her eyes. "It's a sty."

"I'd bet most every parent would say the same thing." Jesse pointed toward both rows of neat bunks. "Camp is different. It's more like fun than work. Besides, everyone is doing it."

"So Mickey's neatness isn't going to automatically continue when he gets home?" Sara asked hopefully.

"Hell, no!"

"Didn't think so."

The rain pounded on the roof of the uninsulated cabin, and they could barely hear each other's words.

Jesse was about to open the door for Sara, when he paused. "Let me get you one of my coats."

"I'm okay."

"You're shivering." He came back with a leather bomber jacket. "Hope you don't mind a contestant jacket."

He held it for her, and she slipped her arms into it. "Oh, this is nice and warm, but what does it say on it?"

"Like I said, it's a contestant jacket. It's from the PBR last year." He shook his head. "Are you sure you want to do this?"

"Of course."

"Let's do it," he said, ready to dash out with Sara, but she put her cold hands on his chest.

"You don't have to spy on Mickey with me."

"And miss the opportunity to say 'I told you so'? No way."

Sara laughed quietly as they left the cabin.

They crunched on the gravel between the two cabins. "We're going to peek in the window," Jesse said.

"I can't see. The window is up too high."

"I know." He threaded his hands and flexed his knees. "Put your foot in here."

"My sandals are pure mud. It'll get all over your hands."

"C'mon. It'll wash off." Tentatively, she put her foot into his hands. "I'm going to boost you up."

"I can see."

The lightning flashed and something cracked, probably a tree.

"What's Mickey doing?" he said it twice, to be heard over the thunder.

"He's playing checkers with another boy."

"He's not bothered about the storm?"

"Uh, no. He's not. You can let me down now, and you can say 'I told you so.'"

"Let's go someplace dry first," he said, wiping his hands on his jeans, as she jumped to the ground.

As he reached for Sara to steady her, she grinned. "I don't know what I was thinking."

They ran to Bunkhouse 13 and entered the cabin. Jesse led her to a chair by his bunk. She took his coat off and hung it over the back.

Jesse took another chair and looked into her grass-green eyes. "Have you thought of counseling while you're here?"

No answer.

"Sara?"

She picked up her former towel, and wiped some of the rain off. "It was your idea to peek in the windows, Jesse."

"Yeah. It was. So you wouldn't go barging into Bunkhouse 12 and embarrassing Mickey."

"I don't think I would have embarrassed him. He would know that I cared."

"What don't you get about young boys and how they can tease?" he asked. "I was one of them. I gave as good as I got. It can be hurtful, if you're on the receiving end."

"Mickey won't defend himself. He won't talk."

"Exactly!"

"Oh."

"He's having a great time. You saw that. Let him be now. Have your own great time."

"Jesse, I can't remember when I've last had a great time, and I can't remember when I relaxed my vigilance with Mickey."

Her words were angry, defiant maybe. Jesse opened the door to escort her back to her bunkhouse. She couldn't be found here with him.

"Well, Sara, I'm going to change that."

Sara walked with Jesse to her bunkhouse in silence. She didn't care about the rain; she was as wet as she could possibly be.

"Thanks for a nice evening, Jesse." Then she shut the door, almost slammed it, in his face.

So, Jesse was going to change things, huh? Stop her from watching Mickey? Show her a good time? If she was such a mess, why did he want to bother with her?

Why couldn't he just be a bull rider and leave the counseling to someone else?

And that was another thing: Jesse wanted her to see a counselor here.

She'd been to so many, she could tell them what they would eventually say: *There's nothing physically wrong with Mickey. He'll talk when he wants to. Be calm and relax, Sara. Meditate. Do yoga. Take a vacation away from Mickey. You need to refill the well and do something for yourself. Why don't you date?*

But right now she just wanted to scream. Hurrying to her bunk, she dived into it, wet clothes and all. Then she buried her face into her pillow and screamed, again and again.

Sometimes she liked this kind of therapy the best.

The evening had started out like a dream. Dancing with Jesse and sitting by the lake with him. If she closed her eyes, she could remember his kisses and feel her stomach flip at the pleasure.

She even had fun peeking in on Mickey with Jesse.

Then he started preaching to her.

She'd wanted one evening where she didn't have to think about Mickey, and she could just be a woman.

Oh, hell! Wanting to comfort Mickey was her obsession tonight, not Jesse's.

Double hell! She was always obsessing over Mickey.

She'd been to every counselor/therapist/psychiatrist and psychologist in her area. She even saw a priest to help her. And the bull rider told her to go to yet someone else at Camp Care?

Sara needed a vacation from all that for a while. Just for a while.

Much to her embarrassment, she had been rude to Jesse. He meant well, but he had to stop telling her to get therapy. Funds were nonexistent, so it was a moot point these days.

Then there was her goal of a cowboy fling. Judging by Jesse's kisses, she had chosen wisely! Then she had blown it by getting mad and practically slamming the door in his face.

It was time to get rid of her wet clothes and maybe take a hot shower. Sara gathered up a set of new clothes, shampoo, soap and a towel and walked to the women's shower.

But something caught her eye in the window on

the right side of the cabin. There it was again. It was a blur, but it kept appearing. She went closer.

It was Jesse Beaumont. He was jumping up and down in front of the window.

Sara cranked out the window and put her forehead on the screen. Jesse jumped up.

"What on earth are you doing?" she asked.

"Can Sara come out to play?"

She chuckled. "Is it still raining?"

"Some. It's more like mist. Let's go for a walk in the mist. I have an hour before I have to get back to Bunkhouse Lucky 13. Or we could go back to the dance."

She hesitated. Did she really want Jesse's company right now?

The answer was an overwhelming yes!

She found a brush in her purse and ran it over her hair. Then she went back to the window. "I'm too much of a mess to go back to the dance, but I'll go for a walk with you."

"Great!"

Sara couldn't believe how quickly she changed into dry clothes. They might get wet again, but she might as well get rid of the thin sundress, put on warm clothes, and top it all off with a Camp Care–issued, yellow plastic poncho.

I must look stunning.

Jesse stood on one of the steps. She saw him just as she opened the door. His wet shirt clung to him like a coat of paint, and she could see every muscle on his chest.

His jeans clung, too—in all the right places.

"Yeah, I'm even wetter since the last time you saw me."

"That was less than ten minutes ago," she said, closing the door behind her.

"See? I can't live without you."

Sara laughed and moved toward the path that led to the lake. "Let's go to the lake again. It must be magical there now with this mist."

"First, I'd like to check on the horses. See how they weathered the storm."

"Okay."

He took her hand and they walked to the barn. It was close to the rec hall where the party was still hopping. She could hear the music and sang along. Jesse joined in with his low, sexy voice.

They weren't Tim McGraw and Faith Hill, but they were good.

Jesse unlocked the padlock with a key from his pocket, opened the door and took her hand again. The earthy smell of dirt, hay and manure hit her, but it wasn't too awful. She got used to it.

Jesse went to each horse, some thirty of them, checking their legs and rubbing their big bodies. She went from stall to stall with him, standing there, watching him, thirty times.

But she didn't mind. She loved watching Jesse. Sara didn't know a thing about horses other than they were big and scary, but she could tell that Jesse had a way with them. His gentle touch and his deep voice soothed the horses.

"All looks good," Jesse said, then he snapped his fingers. "Let's dance."

"Here?"

"Sure. It has a nice dance floor. Just watch where you're stepping."

She threw her head back and laughed. It was hard to stay miffed at the bull rider.

He held out a hand, and she took it. He twirled her twice before she landed in his arms.

His hand went to her back and she heard the crunch of a poncho. "Sorry, but I left my ball gown back in my cabin."

"I left my tux back in mine."

He twirled her around the barn in step to an old Anne Murray song echoing from the recreation center, covering a lot of barn territory. She was getting dizzy, but she loved it. Sara could picture herself in a beautiful ball gown, and how dashing Jesse would look in a tux.

Lit by overhead lamps, dust motes whirled around them. Periodically, a horse would whinny, reminding her that she had an audience.

And Jesse hummed in her ear. The cowboy sure could move, and she knew that because one of her therapists had suggested that she take ballroom dancing to calm herself. She'd graduated in six weeks, and she wasn't any calmer, but she was a better dancer.

Sara wanted to get rid of the poncho so she could feel the warmth of Jesse's hand on her back, but all too soon the song was over and the next dance was a fast one.

Jesse checked his watch. "I'm sorry about our walk, Sara. I have to get back so Roving Ramrod Ronnie can spend some time at the party. I didn't know that checking the horses would take so long."

"It's all right. I'm getting tired. Tomorrow's going to be a long day, starting with breakfast. We are having hash, scrambled eggs and beans for breakfast. Oh, and sourdough biscuits. It's our Salute to the Trail Ride Day."

"I see." He chuckled. "What's for lunch?"

"Beans and Sloppy Joes on a sourdough biscuit." She grinned. "You know how those drovers loved their Sloppy Joes."

"Dare I ask about supper?"

"Beans—"

"Of course! What else? Oh, please don't say it, don't say it!"

"Chili."

"You said it." He shook his head. "My brother Reed told me that Cookie was big on chili. I'm not a fan of the stuff."

"I'll see what else I can make you."

At first he seemed grateful until he thought about it more. "No. Absolutely not. I'll have what my wranglers are having."

She laughed. "What some ramrods will do for God, country and their wranglers." Sara held up her hand and they high-fived.

"C'mon, I'll walk you home."

"I'm okay. You don't have to walk me back."

"I insist. Maybe this time, you won't slam the door in my face."

"Uh… I was overwhelmed by some…issues."

Jesse locked up the barn behind them, and took her hand. "Any of those issues have to do with me?"

"They're long-standing ones. You just reminded me of them when I wanted to forget them for a month."

"Care to give me more information? You're a little sketchy, and I don't want to make the same mistake."

Sara didn't speak. She was deciding whether or not to share her feelings with Jesse, but she'd never mention a fling with him.

He squeezed her hand. "I have two ears. Hit me with it."

"I just wanted to take a break from counseling, and I just wanted to use the time here for a type of uh…vacation. When I get back to reality, I'm going to have to hunt for a job, and get back into running the two of us from therapist to therapist."

"Gets tiring, doesn't it?"

"I feel like a soccer mom without the ball."

They both laughed.

Sara listened to the rain dripping from the trees. "You know, Jesse. You're good for me, mostly."

"Mostly?"

"I haven't laughed this much in a long time."

"But, Sara, you have a great sense of humor."

"It's been dormant."

"It's waking up," Jesse told her.

Sara could hear laughter coming from up the

path. Some of her bunkmates were returning from the party.

She stepped away from Jesse. No sense in initiating any more gossip than what already existed about her and Jesse.

"Hey, you two," said Jules, one of a group of four, all of whom were her bunkmates. "Did we interrupt something?"

"No," Sara said.

Jesse grinned. "Yes! We were just saying goodbye."

"We'd better leave them alone, ladies," said Patty.

They filed into the cabin single file, giving Sara raised eyebrows and winks.

She couldn't help but grin. Jesse pulled her close. "I'm giving you the opportunity to run away."

Sara longed for some goodbye kisses. "Why would I want to do that?"

"I don't know if I'm part of your vacation plans."

"Cowboy, you are at the top of the list of my vacation plans."

Sara closed the gap between them, putting her hands on his cheeks. She couldn't believe she was that bold.

Jesse raised an eyebrow, waiting patiently for her next move.

She kissed his lips, tentatively at first, then harder. He pulled her close, closer still. Darn the yellow poncho! It was creating a barrier between them.

Jesse must have thought so, too. He pulled up her poncho and placed his hands on her hips.

Then he dipped her!

She wasn't ready for that, and gave a garbled scream. He kissed her, his tongue playing with the outline of her lips. She opened her lips for him, and his tongue found hers in an intimate dance.

All too soon, he righted her, and she gasped for breathe.

"What was that?" she asked.

"A dip."

"Do it again, Jesse."

And he did.

Chapter 9

Sara stifled a yawn the next morning as she was dishing out hash and scrambled eggs in the chow line. Jules, next to her, had the pancakes. Then Patty had the fruit.

They were all tired because they didn't get to sleep until about four in the morning. Then they had to be at the chuck wagon to help Cookie get breakfast ready at six.

The laughing and teasing in her bunkhouse had been one for the record. It was as if she was back in a pajama party circa eighth grade and talking non-stop about boys.

There was chat about first dates, ex-husbands, current husbands, the one who got away, but the most gossip revolved around one man: Jesse Beaumont.

"You should see that man ride bulls," Kelli said. "He's a real cowboy."

"He's also wonderful with the kids in the equine program."

Janice chuckled. "I'm wondering how *I* can get into the equine program."

"If he rescues kittens from trees, I'm in love!" added Jules. "Hell, I'm in love with him now! Sara, you're one lucky woman."

"Sara, is he a good kisser? He has to be," Patty said.

Janice shook her head. "Don't answer that."

Sara raised her hand for them all to stop. "I am afraid that you all are under the wrong impression. We're just friends."

"You looked like more than friends on the steps just now," Janice stated.

"Let's change the subject," Sara said, then raised an eyebrow. "I don't kiss and tell!"

The bunkmates all roared with laughter, but thankfully, the subject changed to one of the roving ramrods by the name of Cooper. Sara remembered Cooper as being tall, dark and handsome, but he had nothing on Jesse.

Sara tried to keep her mind on the job at hand. She searched the chuck wagon line for Mickey, and he was about twentieth in line, patiently waiting.

Finally, it was his turn. "Good morning, Mickey. Are you having fun?"

He nodded enthusiastically and grinned.

"And you are going to ride today, right?" Sara asked.

There was the same reaction, and Sara hoped that Mickey would say something, anything.

Mickey moved along the line, and Sara waited for Jesse to come through. Craning her neck, she didn't see him.

"Waiting for Jesse?" Jules whispered.

"No. Not at all."

"Yeah, right. Sara, it's written all over your face."

"What is?"

"That you're interested in him."

"Jesse and I fight all the time, Jules," Sara whispered, ladling out hash and eggs to the next wrangler. "It's not what you think. I'm just going to have a summer fling, remember?"

"Then fling away," Jules said. "But I think you should hold out for more. The man is a good catch."

"Mickey is my life. I don't have room for a man."

"Yes. Yes, you do, Sara. Of course, you do. Look, we don't know each other very well, but I'd hate for you to miss out on a great opportunity."

"And I have to get to know Jesse more."

"Not for a fling you don't. You just need to know their sexual history. You know, how many partners has he had? Has he been tested?"

Sara dropped her large spoon on the floor. "Oh, no. I never thought about all of that."

She picked up the spoon from the floor, and went over to the sink to wash it. Her stomach sank. She'd never had to think about all that stuff before. Truth be told, Michael had been her only partner, since they grew up together in the same grammar school and high school. They even both went to Syracuse University. Michael got a bachelor's in business, but Sara had had to drop out to work to pay for some of Michael's tuition so he could finish.

She remembered berating Jesse because he was going to community college when he could, when she'd never gone back to SU to finish her degree.

What kind of a snob was she?

Now she had to worry about Jesse's previous sexual partners? She couldn't imagine the number of buckle bunnies throwing themselves at his feet. Jesse had to be a man of steel to resist them. She was going to need an adding machine.

And she hoped like hell that all of his encounters were protected.

She had to talk to Jesse before she got together with him. Added to all that was Mickey… Life sure was complicated.

Maybe she should forget about a fling, and forget about Jesse.

"Hi there, Sara!" It was Jesse. "You're going to scrub a hole in that metal spoon."

She didn't realize that she'd been still washing the spoon while she was thinking. Looking out front, she gasped at the long line. "Can't talk. I have to get back to my station."

"I am at the end of the line, but I came to ask you if you are busy tonight."

"Uh…no." Jesse walked with her as she returned

to ladling out food. "Sorry, Jules. It took longer than I thought."

Jules looked at Jesse and winked. "I'm sure it did."

"No. You don't understand."

"So, Sara, are you busy tonight?" Jesse asked.

"No, but can we talk later?"

"I'll talk to you after Mickey's riding lesson. I know where to find you." He smiled and walked away. She tried not to watch him. Jules and Patty would call her on it.

"I wonder what you're going to do on your date," Jules whispered.

"I don't know," Sara said. "It'll probably be a walk by the lake." The sun shone brightly this morning, and it didn't seem like it would rain. Maybe they would go for a stroll, sit on the rocks and talk.

Her emotions were running the gambit, from worry to excitement and everything in between. She should back off and just keep it cool and casual with Jesse, despite her eagerness to be with him.

Or maybe, as always, she was just making things more complicated than they needed to be.

No matter what, she was looking forward to being with Jesse.

"A horseback ride?" Sara asked Jesse, wide-eyed. He caught her on the path, just as she was ready to duck into her favorite spot, into the cedar trees and the bushes, to watch Mickey's lesson.

"Yes. I thought we'd go for an after-dinner walk."

"You can do that?"

"Who's going to stop me? They're my horses, and they need exercise."

"Your horses, Jesse? I thought they all belonged to Camp Care."

"Most of them belong to the camp, but they needed more mounts this season. There are eight Beaumont horses here especially trained for equine therapy. I brought them on a couple trips in my trailer, over there." He pointed to a massive white trailer at the far end of the tar-covered parking lot. Its logo boasted five *B*'s, and Beaumont Ranch written in big letters, with Beaumont, Oklahoma, under it.

She took her sunglasses off, and cleaned them with the hem of her yellow Camp Care shirt. "I guess I didn't notice it, but how on earth could that be? It's huge, and so is the printing."

"It was behind the barn before, but I moved it. With the rain, it was sinking into the ground."

"Oh."

"So, are you into a trail ride after dinner? We won't go far."

"Jesse, I've never been on a horse. Never. They are big, and scary and tall…and…scary and big and tall."

"But Mickey rides. Are you going to let him show you up?"

"Yes! And Mickey rode only once."

"Today is twice."

"Twice, then." Jesse grinned. "And get out of the bushes, will you please? You can watch the class by the fence. I'll even bring you a chair. Mickey probably won't even notice you're watching."

"Will you pick me out an easy, rocking one, not too small and not too big?"

"A chair?"

"No! A horse. For tonight."

"They are all like that. My horses, I mean. Not a chair." They both laughed. "Gotta go, Sara. My class is arriving. I'll bring you that chair. Over there. By the fence."

He gave her a quick kiss on the forehead, and this time he caught her watching him walk away and grinned. "Caught ya."

"I was looking at the barn," she lied.

"Uh-huh."

After that encounter, Sara's mind was whirling, and at the same time, her stomach was churning.

She was never going to wash her forehead again.

She needed to ask Jesse about his sexual history.

Jesse caught her watching him walk away.

Jesse would bring her a chair to watch Mickey, and she would get out of the bushes. She'd be spider-free.

She was going to ride a horse after her supper shift.

Jesse walked out of the barn with a rocking chair over his head. He put it down in front of her. "Just as you requested."

"Thanks, Jesse."

"When you're done, leave it there, and I'll put it back."

"Okay."

"Mickey seems to be in good spirits today. He can't wait to get on his horse, but first, a lesson on saddling," Jesse said.

"He'll love it. It's not arithmetic or spelling or reading."

"He doesn't like to read?" Jesse asked.

"Nothing but superhero comic books. As much as I dislike them, at least he's reading something."

Jesse rubbed his chin, as if he were thinking.

"I have to go. Time to start class."

As usual, the class started in the barn, and while she waited, she turned her face up to the sun. It was a fabulously beautiful day. The scent of horses and hay and cedars wafted on the air, and Sara took a deep breath to remember this day forever.

The wranglers came out of the barn helped along by their assistant, who could be an aide or a therapist or a ramrod. There were eight riders in all. Some looked very serious, while some, like Mickey, had nervous smiles plastered on their face. But Jesse wasn't leading him. Jesse stood in the middle of the corral watching each rider like a hawk.

"Whoa!" Jesse said. "Wranglers whoa!" He waited until everyone stopped their mounts. "Wranglers, reverse!"

The ramrods halted, then assisted the wranglers in turning their horses.

"Excellent job, wranglers! Excellent. Wranglers, walk your horses!"

Jesse asked the campers to do another reverse, then said, "I am preparing you wranglers for a trail ride. It's going to be part of the end of the month rodeo! Yeehaw! Let's hear it wranglers!"

"Yeehaw!" said most of the kids.

Sara held her breath, hoping that Mickey would yell, too.

"Wranglers, I can't hear you!"

"Yeehaw!"

Mickey didn't answer, but he did pump the air with his fist. She laughed with happiness. That was as excited as she'd ever seen Mickey. She crossed her fingers that maybe he'd have a breakthrough soon.

"Mickey, keep your hand on the reins, cowboy."

Mickey held the reins so hard, Sara could see that his knuckles were white.

Jesse cupped his hands over his mouth and shouted, "Okay, wranglers, return to the barn and clean your horse's tack. Don't forget to give your horse a carrot from the bin."

Sara liked how Jesse spoke to the kids. He didn't treat them like little boys. Instead, he spoke to them like adults and they rose to the occasion. Every kid got the attention that they needed from Jesse.

The man is hot, Sara thought. Who didn't love a guy who liked kids and animals?

When she wasn't looking at Mickey, she couldn't take her eyes off Jesse. He had a presence that had everyone gravitating toward him. It didn't hurt that he was a sports figure, a top bull rider. This gave him a type of aura that he was tough, that he liked to flirt with danger, and because he downplayed his bull riding, it made him more intriguing.

Sara continued to be intrigued.

She headed to the chuck wagon for her lunch shift. At the same time, Jesse headed for the rec hall. She wondered why he was going there when it was lunchtime.

Sara rolled her eyes. She had to get him out of her head. Who cared that he went to the rec hall? *I do.*

Cookie assigned her to the kitchen to make potato salad, about eighty tons of the stuff! The potatoes were already peeled, but she had to dice them up, add mayonnaise, and mix it all up. Once she finished, she put everything in the walk-in fridge, and went out front to see what else she could do.

Scanning the dining hall, she looked for Mickey. He was sitting next to Jesse, and—*oh, my*—her son was actually reading a book. She couldn't help herself; she walked over to the table, and raised an eyebrow at Jesse.

Jesse looked up at her from his place at the table. "I picked up a copy of *Black Beauty* for Mickey. I thought he'd be interested in it." He gave Mickey a nudge with his elbow. "Since Mickey rides a black horse. Only Mickey's horse is named Socks."

Sara stopped herself from giving Jesse a big hug and an even better kiss for thinking of her son, and going through the trouble of getting the book at the camp library.

Oh! That's where he'd been going, she thought. The camp library was in the rec hall.

"I loved *Black Beauty* when I was a kid." Sara

purposely left out that she'd cried during most of the book, so Mickey would keep reading.

As she looked at Mickey, bent over the book and turning the pages. Her son was riveted in a book that wasn't a superhero comic book. She owed it all to Jesse.

Okay, so score another point for the bull rider.

"So, cowgirl, are we still on for later?"

Her stomach churned when she thought of getting up on a horse. A real horse!

"I think so, but I have to tell you that I am nervous, almost as nervous as when I thought about Mickey getting up on one."

"I promise you that riding a horse is just like rocking in a chair, only you cover some land. I will pick out a perfect horse for you." He raised a palm as if taking a pledge. "Camp Care ramrod's honor."

"Helmet, knee pads, elbow pads and Bubble Wrap included?"

He chuckled. "Absolutely."

She sighed. "Then I guess I'll see you after dinner."

He pushed his white cowboy hat back with a thumb. "Don't sound so excited. You're going to bruise my ego."

"Oh, I think your ego will survive intact."

"What makes you say that?"

"All your buckle bunnies have certainly puffed up your ego to last you at least fifty years."

He whistled. "And how do you know about the… ahem…buckle bunnies that hang around me?"

"The ladies in my bunkhouse filled me in about you, Jesse."

Open mouth, insert foot!

"So, you've been talking about me?"

"Yes. I mean no." Sara's face heated up, and she was sure that she was about to burst with embarrassment. "I mean no. No. Oh, darn it. All right, yes." She couldn't think fast enough to get out of this one.

Jesse raised an eyebrow. "What else have the ladies in your bunkhouse been saying about me?"

Sara raised an eyebrow in return. "That you are as conceited as...as...uh..."

"As the day is long?"

"That works."

Sara wondered if she could actually die of embarrassment. If so, her will was ready and at her lawyer's office, and her aunt Tysia had wholeheartedly agreed to take care of Mickey.

She felt better, but she was out of her comfort zone in flirting with Jesse, if she could call it that.

How could she face him again?

Chapter 10

Jesse didn't have time to eat; he was too busy trying to find a roving ramrod to watch his wranglers for a while.

Jeremy Dixon finally agreed to do it, but Jesse had to promise him two front row seats to the Tacoma bull riding event.

Because he didn't want to ride in the dark with Sara, he'd also arranged with Cookie to release her from her dinner duties. That cost him two tickets to all five days of the PBR World Finals in Vegas in November.

If he'd had the time to negotiate, he would have gotten Cookie to agree to just one or two days, but he had to dash to the barn and get two of his horses saddled, and then head over to the chuck wagon to pick her up. When Cookie saw him at the front porch to pick up Sara, Cookie would surprise her and let her go.

For Sara, Jesse picked out a mare named Midnight. She was a chestnut with four white socks and a white spot on her rump. She was the sweetest and gentlest horse on four horseshoes. Jesse always used Midnight for the kids who were agitated, couldn't sit still or needed a special saddle.

Midnight was comparable to Socks, the horse he'd assigned to Mickey. The Beaumonts had received both horses from a generous neighbor who helped out with the equine therapy on various weekends at the Beaumont Ranch.

As he walked both horses to the chuck wagon, he had to chuckle when he thought about Sara talking herself right into a corner.

The ladies in my bunkhouse filled me in about you, Jesse.

His reputation had preceded him at Camp Care. Sure, he enjoyed the attention of his female fans, and some were more beautiful than others, but he'd never found that special someone.

His brothers had both found special women, and Jesse had never seen Luke or Reed that smitten before. They were even happier building their homes on Beaumont land.

Maybe someday he'd be as crazy in love as those two galoots with their ladies.

Until then, he was enjoying the company of Sara Peterson. She was unlike any woman he'd ever known. She was stubborn, opinionated—mostly about him—and she was like a rose that had been kept under a rock for too long. An unhappy marriage would do that.

Just then, he saw Cookie open the side door of the chuck wagon, and push Sara gently out the door. "Sara, we don't need you tonight," Cookie said. "But Jesse here thinks you need a horse ride."

"*Walk*. A horse *walk*," she corrected. "Are you sure you don't need me, Cookie?"

He puffed up his white chef's hat. "It's a slow night tonight."

"It's the same crowd as every night."

"Go. Have fun with Jesse," Cookie said, turning her toward Jesse and pointing.

Her eyes grew wide. "Can't we walk on foot, Jesse? They are awfully big."

"If your son can do it, you can do it."

"That's too logical. Which one is mine?"

"Midnight."

"I see them!" She grinned. "Boy or girl?"

"Girl."

"Good. Maybe we can bond before she bites me with her big yellow teeth. Yours looks like the one Roy Rogers had."

"Just how old are you?" he joked. "Anyway, mine is called Sunshine. He's a palomino like Trigger."

"Midnight and Sunshine, huh?"

"Yep. Do you want to pet them?"

"I would, but I'm chicken."

"Follow my lead."

She walked down the stairs and tentatively petted Midnight on her face. "She's pretty."

"Want to feed her a carrot?"

"I do."

"Hold it up and out in front of her. She'll be gentle."

All was fine until the carrot shrank to a nub, then Sara panicked. "Now what, bull rider?"

"Hold your palm flat. She'll gently take the carrot."

"Remember that I need all ten fingers to type."

"Shoot, Sara! Some people have typed with less."

"Gee, thanks."

Sara gave both Midnight and Sunshine carrots and an apple. "Are you comfortable to try riding Midnight now?"

"I am if she is."

"She is." He laughed. "Put your left foot in the stirrup, and swing your right leg over the saddle and put it in the other stirrup."

"If I can get up there, do I get a ten from the French judge?"

He chuckled. Sara could be a hoot, or maybe her comical side came out when she was under stress. If that was the case, then he'd be laughing all evening.

"Quit stalling. You want me to help you?"

"No."

Her snippy side came out when she was angry or nervous, like when they'd first met and she found out that he was a bull rider. Jesse still thought that Sara didn't trust him to help Mickey.

If nothing else, the bunkhouse environment was helping Mickey make friends, and Mickey was laughing again. Big belly laughs, and it was music to his ears.

Ty, J.B. and Glen were all close in making breakthroughs. Jesse could feel it.

He could say the same for Mickey, too.

Jesse planned on taking the four boys who didn't talk on a little hike around the lake. Maybe they'd have a campfire, and if nothing else, Jesse could tell them about bull riding.

Returning to the present moment, he snapped his fingers when another brilliant idea crossed his mind.

"What are you thinking, Jesse?" Sara asked.

"I'll tell you later, but if you're done petting the hair off Midnight, we should get riding."

"Walking. The horses are going to walk," Sara insisted.

"Sure."

"I mean it, Jesse. Nothing fancy."

"Of course not. You're a beginner." He was serious, and he meant it. As tame as Midnight and Sunshine were, an animal had a mind of its own.

"Mount up, Sara. I'll help you."

"I can do it myself. I've watched *Gunsmoke* reruns enough times. Mickey is a *Gunsmoke* addict."

"Isn't everyone?" He waited for Sara to get on Midnight while he held the mare still. It took her only four tries, but she finally did it.

"I'm so high up, I can see Canada from here."

"Can you see Calgary, Canada? I've passed up the Calgary Stampede and working on our ranch to come to Camp Care."

"What's that?"

Jesse nodded. She was talking to avoid showing her nerves. But he could appreciate her determination to even give horseback riding a try.

"The Calgary Stampede is several days of events. Rodeos, music, carnival rides, chuck wagon races and, of course, bull riding."

"Sounds like fun."

"It is." He stared up into her green eyes. They were as big as his belt buckles. "Shall I lead Midnight around for a while?"

"Please." Her voice was shaky.

"Relax, Sara. Just relax, breathe and enjoy the ride. I mean…the walk."

He walked the horse on the road to the barn, around the bunkhouse row and then back to get Sunshine.

"Ready to try this on your own?"

"Yes." She smiled nervously and giggled, but at least she wasn't too petrified to react. "It is like rocking in a rocking chair, Jesse."

He handed her both reins. "We'll ride side by side. That way we can talk."

"Okay."

He swung up onto his palomino.

They walked their horses. After several minutes of silence, alternated with giggling and finally the hiccups, Sara turned to Jesse. "Is Mickey still reading?"

"Absolutely. He can't put *Black Beauty* down."

"Thank goodness. I owe you big-time for getting him to read, especially during Camp Care."

"You don't owe me anything."

Sara smiled. "Tell me more about the Calgary Stampede. Did you win the rodeo there?"

"You mean, did I win the bull riding? A rodeo has several events like bronc riding, steer wrestling, steer roping, barrel racing and bull riding. I won the bull riding last year. My brother Reed won it two years ago, and Luke won it three years ago. I won't be able to defend my title this year."

"Why not?"

"Because I'm here at Camp Care."

"Oh, I'm so sorry."

"I'm not," he said, shrugging. "I like being here at Camp Care and being with the kids. I love seeing their faces when they accomplish something that they never thought they'd do in a million years. This is really a great place. I was skeptical at first, but have really come around to admire the program and what they do for kids."

"But you said that you have some equine therapy weekends at your ranch."

"We do. But I usually don't get that involved because the PBR events are on the weekends. But, the kids stay over in our bunkhouse with their chaperones and equine therapist for some weekends scattered throughout the summer. I'd like to expand it someday because we only reach Beaumont County kids. Maybe when I've retired from the PBR, I can expand the program."

Sara nodded, but didn't look at him. She seemed to be relaxing, but she had a death grip on the reins, just like Mickey, and wouldn't look at him, not even a quick glance.

He kept on talking to further get her to calm down and enjoy the ride. "It's a full-time job, organizing everything and making sure that all the releases are signed and whatever. My brother's wife, Callie, does everything. And Callie is busy doing our accounting, making our plane and hotel reservations for the events, and whatever the hell else she does. She can't take on much more, but she insists that she wouldn't give up the Beaumont Ranch Equine Therapy Program for all the help in the world."

"She sounds like a great person."

"Callie is a gem. So is my brother Luke's wife, Amber. She's a full-time cop and is currently pregnant, so she's a bit busy. Callie lets her help out, but not much." He chuckled. "Both my brothers married great women."

"They really sound wonderful."

"That's a perfect way to describe them."

Sara was pretty wonderful herself.

Even though she overdid it sometimes, Sara was like a mother bear with her cub. She worked hard in the kitchen, wasn't too proud to take a scholarship. And she was beautiful, even though she seemingly didn't know it. Above all, she wasn't a buckle bunny. She really didn't even know about bull riding at all.

He'd like to take her to a bull riding event. Or maybe bring one to her.

Jesse reminded himself to talk to Lori Floyd about bringing several bulls to Camp Care. If they had a break from building their houses, maybe he and his brothers and a couple of other cowboys could put on an exhibition here. The Beaumont brothers had the fencing and the bulls, it'd be easy; it could be part of the rodeo at the end of the season.

"Jesse, you never mentioned your parents. How are they?"

"My mother died several years ago." He left out the fact that she had died after being kicked by a horse. Sara didn't need to know that, not when she was a new rider. "And my father fell apart. He's had trouble with drinking, and right now he's on probation for a bar fight."

"Is he doing okay?"

"He's doing great. He lives in town, has a lady friend and comes out to the ranch a lot. He's still pining for my mother, and I think it pains him to be at the ranch, instead of it comforting him."

"Maybe that'll change when Amber gives him a grandbaby."

Jesse nodded. "How about your folks?"

"They're fine. They live in Oregon. I don't see them much, but we talk a lot on the phone."

They walked their horses in comfortable silence until Sara turned to him. "This is really fun, Jesse. I'm so glad you suggested riding."

"Walking," he said, echoing what she'd said earlier. "But I think it's time to go back. I don't want you to ride in the dark. I'll turn and Midnight will follow Sunshine."

"How do I do it?"

"Let the reins go against her neck in the way you want to go." Sara obeyed, and he exclaimed, "That's it! Excellent, Sara!" The horses were trained so perfectly that even first-timers could handle them, but he was also proud of her for confronting her fears.

"I'm riding a horse!"

"You are."

"I have to show Mickey!"

"Maybe we'll see him on our way back."

They talked about the weather, yoga and horses, and when they got back to the barn Jesse led the horses to the corral. One of the workers was there, and Jesse asked her to get Mickey.

Jesse led Sunshine around the corral, and Midnight followed. Mickey arrived, looking surprised. He grinned widely and clapped.

When Jesse looked back at Sara, her green eyes looked like shimmering pools. He assumed it was because of Mickey's reaction. The boy responded to stimulation, and he was doing it more and more.

He was proud of himself. He'd taught two city slickers how to sit on a horse and be comfortable.

He dismounted from Sunshine and then helped Sara off. Touching Jesse's arms, she said, "That's the best reaction I've seen from Mickey in a long time. He's definitely coming alive, and I have you to thank." She leaned forward and kissed him. It was too quick a kiss for him. He wanted more, and maybe she did, too. "Naw. It's the Camp Care environment."

"Maybe, but you are part of the environment, Ramrod Jesse."

He chuckled. "Go and see your son, and I'll be waiting for you in the barn to show you how to brush Midnight and clean tack."

"Okay."

Wanting to see what Sara would do, Jesse slowly walked the horses into the barn, but he watched as Sara fussed over Mickey's hair, combing it with her fingers. The poor kid. He was surrounded by a group of his fellow wranglers, who were clearly trying like hell not to laugh.

If she wet a finger and wiped dirt off his face, Mickey would never live it down.

Oh, no! She started to, but Mickey ducked away. Then he left with his group. Sara looked hurt, but she trudged up to the barn.

"He didn't want me there," she sniffed.

"Sara, you embarrassed him in front of his friends. You're still treating him like a three-year-old."

She put her hands on her hips. "And how many children have you had, Jesse?"

"None. But I was a young boy once, and I saw the reaction of his fellow wranglers just now. Didn't you?"

"Uh…no. I was looking at Mickey."

"Exactly. And I wasn't, so I could see the bigger picture."

She sighed. "I don't want to fight with you, Jesse. Every time we talk about Mickey, we seem to fight."

"We're not fighting. I'm just pointing out that you embarrass the kid in front of his friends. Unless you want your son to avoid you like the plague, stop fussing over him."

He made his tone direct and to the point.

"Just show me what you want me to do with Midnight. I want to go to the chuck wagon and help clean up. I think we are down a dishwasher," she said, her voice expressionless.

Yep. He'd made her mad, but maybe she'd think about what he'd said.

"I'll take care of Midnight for you, so you can help out at the chuck wagon. I'll see you later."

"Thanks." She walked to the side door, then turned back. "And thanks for a great time, Jesse. I mean that."

"Would you do it again?"

Her face brightened. "I would."

"Next time, you can try bull riding."

Sara whirled around. "In your dreams, cowboy."

She had a smile on her face, and hopefully her anger was evaporating. Maybe she'd take his comment for what it was intended to do: help both her and Mickey.

As she walked to the chuck wagon, Sara mumbled, "That man is insufferable. Why can't he just be a cowboy and leave the therapy to those with degrees in that field?"

She was just doing things that a mother would do.

Maybe he had a point. Maybe she was embarrassing him in front of his fellow campers.

Yeah. Okay.

Maybe she should go into Bunkhouse 13 and apologize to Mickey. Yes. That's what she would do. Later, when he was ready for "lights-out."

So, after she was done washing dishes and cleaning up after dinner, she knocked on the door of the bunkhouse. Jesse opened the door widely, then when he saw it was her, he closed it until she could barely see him.

"What's up, Sara?"

"I'd like to see Mickey and apologize."

"Not a good idea. Not now."

"Why not?"

"Because all the boys are in their pajamas, and we are about to have storytelling."

"Then I can't tuck him in? I miss tucking him in."

"Are you insane? Mickey could never hold his head up in this camp, maybe not even this state!"

Sara giggled. "I'm only kidding. This time."

"You gave me a heart attack." He glanced over his shoulder. "Look, let's talk later. The wranglers are waiting for me."

"Can you get a roving ramrod tonight?"

"It's already done. Meet you at the lake for yoga at nine thirty. Bring a lantern."

She was looking forward to it.

Chapter 11

As she walked to her bunkhouse, Sara wondered if she was actually getting her sense of humor back. She'd been at Camp Care only several days, but she hadn't felt this relaxed since the accident.

She even slept through the night. Maybe the scent of cedar in the air was a type of aromatherapy, or maybe it was because she wasn't worrying quite so much about Mickey.

Thanks to Jesse, Mickey was relaxing, too. Okay, perhaps her constant vigilance in the past had made her son edgy, so it was good that they were apart a little. Just a little.

Then she remembered how Jesse got *Black Beauty* out of the camp's library for Mickey, and how Mickey was still reading it.

What a blessing! Maybe she was just getting the wrong books for him, but they were recommended by the librarian for his age group. They sat unopened on the desk in his room.

If she tried reading aloud to him, she received eye rolling in return. Okay, maybe he was too old to be read to.

But Mickey was only ten years old. He was still her baby.

Jesse would disagree with her. He'd tell her to leave him alone and let him grow up.

Sara opened the door of her bunkhouse, and was greeted by raucous noise, which stopped when she walked through the door.

"What?" Sara asked.

"We saw you riding with Jesse Beaumont," Jules said.

Tiffany said, "Everyone's talking about how the two of you are always together."

Sara shook her head. "Jesse is just helping me with Mickey. He's gotten him to read."

"He's helped me with my J.B., too, but he's never taken me riding with him."

Meghan yelled over the noise that erupted, "The same goes for my Ty. I'd love to go riding with Jesse. No. I'd just want to stand there and look at him,"

Sara grabbed her Camp Care sweatshirt and shrugged into it. "Don't wait up, ladies." She grinned. "Jesse and I are going to do yoga." She purposely got them talking again, and wasn't disappointed with the results.

"So that's what they call it these days," Meghan laughed and the rest of the bunkhouse chimed in.

Once Sara got to their place by the lake, which gave her a chance to relax and meditate, she couldn't clear her mind. Thoughts of Jesse whirled through her.

Fling. She wanted to have a fling. Just lovely, meaningless sex without any ties.

Jesse had a reputation for being a party boy, so why couldn't they have their own party together? Alone.

They did share some wonderful kisses by the water, but Sara wanted much, much more.

Then they would continue with their own lives when July was over.

Her life would be devoted to finding another job, trying to pay for the roof over their heads and going to counseling alone and with Mickey. Jesse would go back to his ranch and the PBR. She hoped he'd win the Finals. It clearly meant so much to him.

She felt bad that he was going to miss the Calgary Stampede. That showed how dedicated he was to Camp Care and to completing his community service.

A twig snapped and she heard, "Sara, it's Jesse. Don't be alarmed."

Her heart did a flip in her chest, not because she was scared, but because it was Jesse.

Sheesh. She was getting to be a buckle bunny!

"I'm fine, Jesse. Just doing some meditating."

"Sorry to disturb you."

"You didn't. Not at all. I really couldn't concentrate."

He smiled, and she could see his bright white teeth by the glow of the lantern. "What are you thinking about? Something bothering you?"

"Nothing much," Sara shrugged. "Just my past, present and future."

"Nothing much? That's just your whole life!"

Along with her thoughts, she waved his words away. She wasn't about to tell Jesse that she was aiming to have a fling with him. "Let's do yoga. You lead this time."

"You might be sore from your ride, so let's shake it off," Jesse said.

They did several poses and Sara sneaked glances at Jesse in his boots, jeans, long-sleeved shirt and cowboy hat. It made her smile and feel flushed at the same time.

"That's it, Sara."

"Awesome. I feel great, and this is a wonderful place to do yoga and meditate." She looked at the sparkling lake and smelled the air, laden with cedar and moisture. "And, Jesse, it's nice to be here with you."

"Thanks."

"I mean it." And she did. It wasn't as if she was flirting; she really liked his company. She might as well tell him just that. "I like doing yoga with you, too," she added, sitting on the big rock next to Jesse.

He stared deep into her eyes, and she thought she

was going to melt. She remembered their kisses here the other day.

"I'm going to kiss you, Sara. If you have any objection, you'd better tell me now."

His low, sexy voice heated her face, her whole body. She was glad that she was sitting, or her legs wouldn't hold her up.

"No objection," she said.

His soft lips met hers, and she kissed him back, tentatively at first, then she put her heart and soul into it.

"Mmm..." Jesse murmured.

He traced her lips with his tongue, and she opened her mouth for him.

They soon both came up, gasping for air. Sara backed away, smiled and then pulled him to his feet. This time, she initiated the kiss, and couldn't keep her hands still. They traveled across his back, threaded into his hair and cupped his face.

"Sara. Wow!"

"Wow! Just what I was thinking."

With their arms around each other, Jesse moved them both down again, to the soft, damp grass. Sara could feel every hard muscle of his body. His heavy belt buckle pressed against her stomach. She groaned.

He played with a piece of her hair. "Jesse, it's been such a long time. I—I..."

"It doesn't matter." He kissed her again, his hand cupping the back of her head.

"What if someone sees us?" she whispered.

He nuzzled her neck. "They all go to the dock at the other end of the lake to hang out."

Suddenly, Sara didn't care if they were caught. She just didn't want Jesse to stop kissing her neck.

She felt his hand under her Camp Care sweatshirt, warming her stomach, then higher. His palm settled on her breast, and she felt dizzy. She wanted to feel his hands on her bare breasts.

Sitting up, she pulled her yellow sweatshirt over her head. The cool night air hit her heated skin, and she shivered.

"Cold?" Jesse asked.

"No. Not at all."

"But you shivered."

"But not from the cold."

"Yeehaw!" He took his hat off, and tossed it nearby. "Come here, Sara."

And she did.

Before Jesse shrugged out of his jeans, he took out his wallet and pulled out a square packet. He tossed his wallet and his jeans near his hat. His formfitting underwear looked like a pair of shorts. They were red with white stripes, and Sara laughed.

"What? You don't like my underwear?"

"They look perfect for Santa Claus."

"Let's see yours." With an index finger, he pulled at the waistband of her jeans, and she couldn't wait to get rid of them.

She sighed, reached for the snap, but he stilled her hand. "Let me."

Leaning on an elbow, he popped the snap, and

slowly—oh-so-slowly—he unzipped her jeans, one rung at a time. She could have screamed, he was taking so long.

She slid off her pants.

"Those are sexy," he said. "Black lace. Nice."

Fancy lace bikinis and lacy bras might have seemed unnecessary to her before because no one but Sara would see them since Michael's death, but they made her feel good when she needed a boost.

Jesse kissed a path up her stomach to her bra, then pulled the straps down.

"More," she whispered.

"I know what you want."

He kissed the mounds of her breasts and bared them to the cool night air.

"Beautiful," he murmured.

He teased a nipple with his tongue, then he gave the other equal attention.

Beautiful? Sara felt like she was having an out-of-body experience. This couldn't be her, making love on the grass with a hunk of a cowboy, a gentle bull rider who was so great with her son.

She wanted to feel his weight, his naked body, on her.

He tugged on her underwear. "You, too, Sara."

She got the message.

Sliding out of her bikinis and bra in record time, she waited not-so-patiently as he opened a condom with his teeth.

"Sara?"

She knew what he didn't ask, what he wanted, what she wanted.

"I want you, Jesse."

They kissed, and she glanced down and saw how hard and big he was.

He was about to slide the condom down his hard length, when she asked, "Can I do that?"

He clenched his teeth and took a deep breath. "Sure."

Sara felt dizzy, drunk, like she was about to faint. Was this an estrogen rush or a sexual high? Whatever it was, she didn't want it to stop.

He pulled her on top of him, and handed her the condom. She had to sit up and straddle his legs.

Rolling the sheath down his erection was the sexiest thing she'd ever done in her life. She felt like a woman again, a participant, and not just an object.

Jesse grunted, and said, "Don't move, Sara, or this is going to be over before it starts."

Grinning, she knew she was actually turning Jesse on! She didn't want to compare him with Michael in the least—that was unfair—but making love with Jesse was...fun, and hot, and...she just didn't have the words to describe it.

In one smooth motion, he pinned her under him. He kissed her gently, and it almost brought tears to her eyes.

"Spread your legs for me," he whispered.

"I want you, Jesse. Now. Hurry!" If he didn't get moving, she was going to explode.

He chuckled. "Let's take it slow."

"In your dreams, cowboy!"

When he slid into her, and they began moving together, Sara wondered if sound would carry, since the lake was so close. If so, all of Camp Care would hear her scream in pleasure.

Jesse smiled down at her, and sighed. "Enjoying yourself?"

"You know I am. You?"

He grunted, nodded and waited for her to catch up.

And they reached the pinnacle together, and slowly drifted back to earth. Sara didn't know when she'd felt so thoroughly sated, so happy and joyful after sex. She'd been a willing participant and she felt sexy and cared for.

Then the fire sirens blared. The real ones. They were coming from Camp Care.

"Hurry! Get dressed, Sara! We have to go!"

Sara's heart beat fast and frantically in her chest. She had to get to Mickey. The sirens were so loud, she couldn't even think.

Stumbling up the path to the camp shoeless and without underwear, she was grateful for Jesse's help that kept her upright and running.

Staff were scurrying toward the wrangler bunkhouses.

"Where's the fire?" Jesse asked a man running by.

"Don't know yet."

"Sara, all ramrods and rovers were assigned tasks in case of a fire. The information area is the recreation hall. Let's go there."

They both were out of breath when they got there.

"Lori…where did it start?" Jesse asked.

"Bathhouse. The one between 12 and 13."

"Were any kids in that bathhouse?" Sara asked Lori.

Lori nodded. "But they're okay. Everyone is okay. It was an electrical fire. The boys ran and told a ramrod. Mickey was one of them. The ramrods who were present handled everything. Right now, the Beaumont County Fire Department is on their way to check on things."

"Where's Mickey?" Sara asked Lori.

"All the wranglers are back and settled in their respective bunkhouses."

Sara turned to leave. "I have to see my son." She took off at a run.

Jesse ran after her. "Wait!"

She ran as fast as she could, trying to ignore the stones digging into her bare feet. She was just about to open the door to Bunkhouse 13, when Jesse put his hand on the door and held it shut.

He took a deep breath and let it out. "Think about what you are going to do and say. Remember, his peers are living with him, and they are going to watch your every move and watch Mickey."

"Other mothers are here with their sons on scholarships, and they—"

"They are not my concern right now, Sara."

"What? I just want to make sure Mickey is okay."

Jesse held his palms up in the air. "He's okay.

Didn't you hear Lori Floyd say that none of the kids were hurt?"

"I want to look at him."

"How about if I get him and send him out?"

"Would you?"

"Make it quick, Sara. Tonight we are going to talk more about the Cowboy Code."

"Thank you." Right or wrong, she wanted to see Mickey for herself.

Jesse opened the big wooden door to the bunkhouse and stepped inside. Sara heard Jesse shout over the yelling and talking from the boys. "Wrangler Mickey Peterson, can I see you for a minute?"

Sara could hear Mickey running down the squeaky plywood floor.

"Mickey, your mom wants to see you outside," he whispered.

The door opened, and Mickey walked out onto the steps.

Sara wrapped him in a hug. Then moved away and studied him. "Mickey, are you all right? Are you hurt?"

He shook his head. Then he put his hand on the door to go back inside.

She was relieved that Mickey was okay, but she was annoyed with herself that she had been off with Jesse when it had happened. She'd never forgive herself if something serious had happened to her son.

She wanted to spend more time with him, have him communicate with her with yes or no answers, but Jesse was probably right. Darn it. Let the boy go.

"Mickey, are you sure you're okay?" she asked, looking him over again.

Mickey nodded, then with a wave goodbye he disappeared through the door.

"Sara, listen at the door," Jesse said.

"Who was that, Mickey, your mommy?" she heard someone say. The question was followed by loud laughter.

Jesse raised an eyebrow at her, then stuck his head back into the bunkhouse. "Okay, wranglers. Get out your copy of the Cowboy Code, and read it again. Oh, and Ronnie the Roving Ramrod, you can go now. I'll take over."

He turned his attention back to her. "That ought to keep them busy."

"You know, Jesse, if we weren't doing yoga and uh…making love out by the lake, you would have been here when the bathhouse caught fire."

"Ronnie the Rover was here. He apparently took care of it efficiently. What's your point?"

"My point is…oh, I don't know…you should have been with your wranglers, and not with me."

"So, we ramrods don't get a break?"

"You've had a lot of breaks already," she said. Maybe she should just keep quiet. She was digging herself into such a big hole she might not be able to get out.

Ronnie the Rover opened the door and stood on the top step. "I wrote some notes in your ramrod logbook. Mostly about the fire. The kids were all okay, and in fact, some of them even alerted staff. That'd be J.B., Ty and Mickey. They are Camp Care heroes."

Sara felt as if a bolt of lightning went through her. "Mickey is a hero?"

"Yes, ma'am," Ronnie said.

"Did he talk?" she asked hopefully.

"No, ma'am. He tugged at my arm."

The lightning fizzled. "Maybe he'll talk soon," Ronnie said.

Ronnie the Rover nodded, and turned to Jesse. "Will you need me tomorrow night?"

He looked at Sara and didn't crack a smile. His sky blue eyes were stormy. "No, but thanks anyway, Ronnie. I've had a lot of breaks already."

Chapter 12

Sara let the hot shower rain down on her later that night. Her feet were filthy, cut and bruised, so she sat down on the little chair provided in the stall and soaped them up.

Okay, maybe she was wrong in telling Jesse that he had a lot of time off, especially when he was spending the time with her.

She owed him an apology.

Her thighs were sore from riding Midnight and from making love with Jesse. She thought about how gentle he'd been, and how much fun lovemaking could be. Adding more cold water, she turned her face up to the shower and let it cool her heated skin.

And she hated to admit it, but Jesse was right about not calling Mickey out of the bunkhouse. His fellow wranglers heard her and teased him—that made her feel horrible—but for heaven's sake, she had to see for herself that he was all right.

Maybe she should just give in and listen to Jesse. Maybe she hovered too much over Mickey. If she wasn't working off a scholarship, she'd be back in Henderson Falls, and would never know what Mickey was doing and therefore she wouldn't fret over him.

Yes, she would.

Her therapists had all told her to give Mickey some time and space, and maybe then he'd talk. Easy for them to say when the boy saw his father die. The first officer at the scene said that he'd heard Mickey screaming, but by the time he got to Mickey's side, he'd stopped and wouldn't answer his questions.

Post-Traumatic Stress Disorder. PTSD. Mutism. She hated those words, those letters, that diagnosis.

And Jesse had the nerve to think that he could help Mickey with his horses, with *Black Beauty* and the Cowboy Code. But she had to admit that he was right about a couple of things.

Sara turned off the water and grabbed her towel. She felt better, although a little cranky. Drying off, she sighed and made a resolution to listen to Jesse… sometimes.

As Sara swept the floor of her bunkhouse, she had time to think.

A week had slogged by since the fire, and Sara hadn't seen much of Jesse, and they'd barely spoken to one another. Sara didn't know if anything was really wrong between them; they were both just busy.

She hated to think that he was the type to be mad and not say anything, but she wanted to clear the air.

Sara got up, worked the three meals, and in between, she watched Mickey ride. She was pleased to see Mickey still reading *Black Beauty* during meals, but she really wanted him to interact more with the other boys.

But that was okay. She was grateful to Jesse for everything.

She was also grateful for the fact that Jesse had showed her how to make love. Slow and joyful was Jesse's version of sex.

With Michael, it had almost seemed as if he didn't know she was even there. It was quiet and quick and left her unsatisfied. Jesse had left her both completely satisfied and wanting to make love with him again.

Every time she saw him in the food line, or walking around Camp Care, she couldn't take her eyes off him. She felt his gaze on her, too.

But considering what they'd shared, small talk in her food line wasn't what she wanted now. She wanted…darn…she didn't know what she wanted. Maybe she longed to make love with Jesse again.

A summer fling just wasn't for her. She decided that she wasn't the type.

Again, it crossed her mind that Jesse might be mad at her. Sara didn't think so, but she never apologized to him for his being right on several counts, and she was being so stubborn.

Jesse seemed to be the type to come right out and tell her if he was mad.

You've had a lot of breaks already.

What a stupid thing to say since Jesse had spent most of his breaks with her. He didn't even come to their favorite spot and do yoga anymore on the grass where they'd made love.

And she missed him.

The next time he came through in the food line, she was going to ask Jesse to meet her at "their place"… tonight.

There were two more weeks left of July, and Jesse had been busy arranging for the rodeo at the end of the season. His brothers agreed to transport several bulls here and the three of them would perform an exhibition—for the staff and the wranglers.

Jesse was going to have Bunkhouse 13 do an exhibition of horse riding. Mickey on Socks would lead the way.

He had plans for the other bunkhouses, but he needed to work with them more.

And he'd been so busy, he barely had time to eat and sleep and talk to Sara. He missed their yoga on the grass above the lake. Hell, he wanted to talk to her and make love with her again.

Maybe someday Sara would really understand how she had been hovering over Mickey because of the car accident.

Mickey was all she had, and Jesse understood why Sara acted the way she did with her son, but it wasn't right. The boy needed to grow, needed some space, and, above all, he needed more friends.

Jesse had told her all that, but she just got mad.

Jesse lost his mom at a young age. When his father crawled into a liquor bottle, which he'd just recently come out of, it was like Jesse had lost him, too. Mickey lost his father to a horrific accident at a real young age. It was like Sara had lost her son. He could understand the struggle, the pain, the feeling of being lost and struggling to find balance. He got that all, but Sara needed to let Mickey grow a little, let him interact with his peers, let him live and enjoy life, and that was also exactly what she needed to do herself.

Now, how was that evaluation from a cowboy who was trying to get a degree in animal husbandry and ranch management?

He couldn't take all the credit. He'd read the file inside and out on all his wranglers, but particularly Mickey.

He checked his watch. Dinner was in a couple of hours. He was going to do some talking with his wranglers, and when he went through the line that night, he'd make arrangements to have some private time with Sara.

After the flag-raising ceremony and the Pledge of Allegiance that morning, Bunkhouse 13 was called to dinner first because the rovers had deemed them the Honor Bunkhouse today, the neatest of them all.

Usually, Jesse would let his wranglers go first, but he wanted some time to talk to Sara.

"Since I nagged you wranglers to clean your areas, I think I should be at the head of the line," he announced, then heard a chorus of objections.

"Awww…that's bogus!"

"Totally bogus!"

"But, Jesse, we did all the work!"

Jesse laughed. "I'm the ramrod, and what I say goes! Now get behind me, and make a nice line."

There was more good-natured grumbling and big smiles from his wranglers who didn't speak.

He could see it on their faces that they wanted to join in the group that was teasing him, but nothing.

But Jesse wasn't going to give up. In his opinion, his nonverbal boys were on the verge of a breakthrough, and that included Mickey.

The door to the chuck wagon opened, and he could see Sara at the first station. She was probably dishing out scrambled eggs.

Their eyes met, and she smiled. That did his heart good. She was glad to see him.

"Wranglers, give this cowboy some room."

There were some kissing sounds from the boys, and Jesse gave them a stern look. Mickey's eyes twinkled. The boy knew that Jesse's objective was to talk to his mother.

Jesse quickly closed the distance between them.

"Sara—"

"Jesse—"

"Go ahead," Sara said.

"Can we meet to talk?" Jesse said.

"Absolutely. That's just what I was going to ask you," Sara said. "For some time."

"Our yoga spot? After dinner?"

"About seven," Sara added.

Jesse nodded. "See you then."

Jesse motioned to his wranglers to go through the line, and again he was subjected to kissing noises.

"'Bout time, Jesse."

"Jesse's in love with Mickey's mother."

Jesse held up a finger. "Knock it off."

When he looked at Mickey, the boy looked surprised, but not displeased by the idea of his ramrod with his mother.

Talk, Mickey. Just talk.

"Hi, sweetheart," Sara said to Mickey, as she ladled eggs onto his plate. "You have your book, huh?"

He nodded.

Mickey had *Black Beauty* with him. He was almost done with it, and sometimes, Jesse could see his eyes beginning to water while reading some of the story.

That touched Jesse. Mickey was in there somewhere, but he was still traumatized due to the accident. Jesse would give all the bulls and cattle on Beaumont land, if only Mickey would talk.

How quickly he'd come to care about this little family! He really enjoyed spending time with them both and wondered if he'd found with Sara what both of his brothers had found with their wives.

The rest of the wranglers were let in, and the noise

level rose considerably. Jesse spent his breakfast eating and watching Sara.

Why was he so attracted to Sara? She wasn't exactly his type. His type was usually the buckle bunnies who came in and out of his life. He partied at the honky-tonks with them. He boot scooted. He flirted and tossed down enough beer to float a battleship.

Yet he was drawn to Sara Peterson. She worked hard, was someone with whom he constantly disagreed, with whom he had heated discussions.

And then they did yoga together and they made love.

If the fire alarm hadn't sounded, he would have gathered her in his arms and held her until daybreak, watching sleep overcome her.

Here he was being poetic when bull riding was his thing, not poetry.

He couldn't wait to talk to her tonight, but until then, he had to settle for watching her dish out food in the chow line and her observing Mickey's riding lessons.

Jesse checked the clock on the wall. It was only eight thirty in the morning. He had to wait until seven thirty at night to talk with Sara.

It was going to be a long day.

When Sara arrived at their spot that night, Jesse was already meditating. Cookie had been messier than usual, so Sara and the other ladies had had a lot to clean up after the chicken, corn, mashed potatoes and gravy dinner.

Jesse had come though her dinner line, and ordered dark meat chicken, her favorite, too. She added a few more pieces on his plate; after all he was a ramrod, and was entitled to an extra helping.

When Mickey came though, she gave him a big piece of chicken breast and put enough gravy on his plate so that his meat was floating.

All of the other campers got their special requests, if those were within reason.

She sat down next to Jesse, but wasn't able to meditate. There was too much on her mind.

Where should she start?

After a while, Jesse spoke. "Can't get into the mood, huh?"

"I want to apologize to you for—"

He put his index finger to her lips. "You don't have to. I get it."

"But—"

"Apology accepted, Sara."

"Okay. That was easy."

"How about a swim?" he asked.

Sara hesitated. It was cold, but maybe Jesse would keep her warm. Now that she had a taste of spontaneity, she liked the feeling.

Why stop now?

"Um… Jesse, uh… I don't have a swimsuit with me."

He had already stripped down to his underwear. This time they were tight-fitting black boxers.

Jesse took her hand and headed for the water's edge. "Don't think. Just do it."

He let go of her hand long enough for her to strip down to her bra and panties. Red lace on both counts. To anyone passing by, it might look like a swimsuit. Not!

"We'll just run in. No getting used to the water slowly. Let's go!" he said.

Hand in hand they kicked up a splash of water, and when the lake had pulled them in, they stopped.

"It's just as cold as I thought it would be," Sara said, thinking that her nipples were so hard they could cut glass.

Jesse put his arms around her and kissed her. His lips were cool, hard and demanding, and she knew that they were going to make love on the bank of Lake Care again.

She'd hoped they would.

"Who's your roving ramrod tonight?" she mumbled.

"Sara…" The tone of his voice warned her not to confirm that Mickey was being supervised tonight.

"Never mind."

"I thought you'd say that."

Jesse floated on his back, and his private parts seemed like they were having a great time saluting the sunset. Sara laughed.

"What?"

She pointed.

Jesse lifted his head and got to his feet, and laughed with her.

"Your turn," he said.

She closed her eyes, kicked her feet, and floated on the lake as if it were a big bed.

Jesse pointed to her, floating on top of the water.

He laughed, and she righted herself. She didn't know if she should wait until he made the first move, but who cared? Slipping out of her bra, she wrapped her arms around Jesse. She wanted to feel her naked breasts against his strong, bare chest.

When Jesse groaned, she felt bold and tugged at his boxers. He got the message and slipped out of them.

"I hope our clothes float," she said. "I'd hate to be caught naked in here."

"You're not naked yet." His voice was low, smooth, sexy and his hands were on the waistband of her panties. She lifted each leg, and he helped her with the thin lace. Then he held her tight.

Sara could feel his hardness pressing against her stomach as he kissed her neck.

"Jesse, I want you. Now."

"Dammit. I don't have a condom with me."

Oh, my. What should she do?

She said a quick prayer that she'd never be pregnant, jobless and maybe homeless. Sara needed to job search when she got back home, and didn't know how long she could stay in her apartment. Mickey and she might have to find something cheaper. She could probably get unemployment insurance, but she'd have to stretch that.

What if she got pregnant with Jesse's baby? Jesse, who rode bulls for a living. Sure, he was a rancher, too, but his…uh…profession was the most danger-ous of all.

She couldn't. She just couldn't.

"I'd give my last dollar to know what you are thinking right now," Jesse said.

"I'm thinking that you need to hustle out of this lake, find your wallet and get protection, or we should put our clothes back on and go to the big bonfire with the rest of the staff and wranglers."

He raised an eyebrow as he played with a nipple. She couldn't breathe, couldn't think.

"How do you vote, Sara?"

"I think we could do both. Now get going and get that condom."

Jesse walked out of the lake naked, as if he didn't have a care in the world. Sara smiled. Jesse was built: muscled, tight butt, strong back and thick thighs. That had to be from riding bulls.

It was nice to see a guy so comfortable in his own skin. Michael had always wondered what people thought of him and was always seeking everyone's approval—everyone except hers. He'd never done anything spur-of-the-moment.

Sara dived into the water to erase thoughts of Michael. He wasn't there to defend himself, and she didn't want to think bad thoughts of him. Michael had given her Mickey.

He'd also made Mickey silent.

Yes. She blamed him for having the accident that made Mickey go inside himself.

She surfaced from her dive, thinking how Jesse

hadn't helped Mickey to speak yet, and he had been all blustery and confident in the beginning.

Jesse had only two weeks left of Camp Care, then he'd be going back to his ranch and soon the PBR would start up.

She was going to miss him once they both left.

Jesse jogged back into the water, then dived in. The silver packet was in his mouth.

"Got it. And I cooled down." Jesse looked down at his groin.

Sara playfully quipped, "Let's see what I can do about that, cowboy."

Chapter 13

The bonfire had dwindled to a campfire when Jesse and Sara arrived. There was clapping and the usual smooching noises coming from his wranglers. He really should have a talk with them about showing some class.

He had heard the gossip about Sara and him. Everyone must think that it was a summer romance, and maybe they were right. However, he wanted to see more of Sara…and Mickey, too, when this session of Camp Care was over. He liked them both. A lot.

But he lived in Beaumont, Oklahoma, and she lived in the middle of New York State. When would they see each other? Maybe Sara could travel to a PBR event or two when the circuit came near her.

The PBR traveled to Madison Square Garden in New York City in January, so that would be a possibility.

Seemed like an awful lot of travel for Sara and Mickey just to see him…well, him and the PBR event.

That was too much to ask.

He could always fly to Syracuse, which was the airport nearest Sara and Mickey. Then he'd rent a car and drive the hour and a half to Henderson Falls. He'd already looked it up.

Yes, he'd do that when his schedule permitted. When PBR resumed at the end of August he'd be busy until Christmas. Plus, there were things to do at the ranch.

There were always things to do there. They had an outstanding staff, but he and his brothers worked every moment they could. But now, with his siblings newly married and building their houses, they wouldn't have much time to help him.

Maybe he had more interest in Sara than she had in him, but he didn't think so.

He'd bet his best saddle that Sara liked him—a lot. The feeling was mutual.

In fact, he liked Sara more than a lot.

Jesse was thinking that he loved her.

He turned to Sara. She looked like she was enjoying the campfire, and was singing along to the silly song. Her head was turned to the right, as if something caught her interest.

Mickey.

Jesse saw that her son was enjoying himself, too.

His fellow wranglers were elbowing one another, elbowing Mickey. Jesse could guess what that was about—Sara and him.

It was unfortunate that Mickey had to be teased because of Jesse's relationship with Sara.

To Jesse's surprise, it looked like Mickey was tolerating the kidding, but he decided to talk to Mickey in the near future.

Like now.

"Sara, I'm going to talk to my wranglers about their kissing noises, and while I'm at it, I'm going to speak with Mickey about our…uh…um…relationship."

"I should do that. Why didn't I think about talking to Mickey?"

"Sara, you're a great mother. I just thought about it before you did. Don't worry."

"I'll go with you."

"I wanted to make it a man-to-man or a ramrod-to-wrangler talk. How about if you speak to him later? Or we speak to him together, later."

She hesitated. "Okay."

Jesse thought that it was probably hard for Sara to wait, and even harder for her to let him handle things. This was a gigantic step for her. Finally, she trusted him and was listening to him.

Jesse approached his wranglers. "Bunkhouse 13. Follow me." He motioned for them to follow him, and they did, to a spot with a large fallen tree.

"Sit down, wranglers." He waited for a moment until he had their attention. "No more kissing noises, please. Respect your ramrod and do unto others as you'd like them to do to you." He was just about to say *respect his lady*, but he'd rather talk to Mickey first. Besides, the Golden Rule covered everything.

"Okay. If there are no questions, you can return to the campfire," he instructed, but when Mickey passed by him, he put his hand on the boy's shoulder. "Mickey, got a minute?"

Mickey nodded.

"Then please sit down again." After the boy did so, Jesse sat down next to him.

"Mickey, I know you're taking a lot of kidding because I've been with your mother, but I like her, and I think she likes me. We are having a good time here at Camp Care. I took her riding, and plan to do it again. We're doing yoga together and meditating together. I'm showing her a lot of things that she hasn't seen in Henderson Falls."

That last sentence could have more than one interpretation, but he hadn't intended it that way!

"Know what I'm going for here, Mickey?"

The boy nodded seriously.

"I like your mother, and I like you, too. I like all my wranglers." Jesse added, "Since you're the man of your family, is it okay with you if I keep dating her?"

Mickey met his eyes, and was so serious that Jesse respected the boy.

Mickey nodded, but raised his index finger.

Jesse waited for him to speak. *Please say something, Mickey.*

He didn't.

"I promise that I'll take care of her, Mickey. Oh, and one more thing—your mom wants to talk with you, too. Later, sometime."

Mickey put his finger down, stood and proceeded to the campfire.

Jesse walked with him. He went to his spot next to Sara, and Mickey went back to the wranglers of Bunkhouse 13.

Mission accomplished.

Operation Sara was yet to come.

The time is flying by much too fast, Sara thought to herself.

In a week, they'd be packing up to leave Camp Care, and she'd be saying goodbye to Jesse.

They discussed how to keep in touch when the week was over, but the logistics and their free time was the problem. Plus, she was panicking because she had to find a job—a job that paid enough so she and Mickey didn't have to move.

So, she guessed that she'd had a summer fling after all.

She could see the sadness in Mickey's eyes, when he came through the food line. He didn't want to leave here, either.

Jesse did a lot of good for his wranglers, though none of the nonverbal kids had started talking.

Before Sara had gotten to know Jesse, she'd blamed him for having zero credentials to be a ram-rod. She had since learned that Jesse had in fact stood on his head to break through to the wranglers who didn't speak.

In attempts to get Mickey to speak, Jesse gave Mickey a lot of attention. Actually, he'd paid a lot of attention to all the wranglers, not just those in Bunkhouse 13. He loved kids.

Jesse was quite a man. And Sara liked him; she really liked him.

After dinner, Jesse showed up again with Midnight and Sunshine. Cookie dismissed her when Jesse popped his head in the kitchen.

"Go, Sara. We're just about done in here. We can handle the rest," Cookie said.

"Yes. Go. Have fun," Jules said. Sara gave Jules a hug.

She'd miss everyone in her bunkhouse, but especially Jules. They had already decided to keep in touch on a group chat.

"When are your brothers coming with the bulls?" Cookie asked Jesse.

"Later today, around four o'clock."

"I might wait to serve dinner. The whole camp wants to watch you cowboys unload them." Cookie laughed. "Me, too."

Jules looked at Sara. "Are you going to watch?"

"Absolutely. The only bull I've ever seen was in a zoo."

Jesse laughed.

Sara raised an eyebrow. "I'm not kidding. He was at the Syracuse Zoo."

Jesse grinned at Sara. "Remind me, and I'll let you pet one."

"Uh…no, thanks. I'll be fine far, far away."

They walked out the back door to their waiting horses. Now that her fear about them had tamped down, Sara could stop and see the beauty of the animals.

She pulled out two carrots from the pocket of her windbreaker. "Courtesy of Cookie."

Feeding Midnight first, Sara petted the animal's large face. The horse was so pretty. Then she ran her hands down the side of the horse's neck. So soft.

She gave Sunshine the same treatment.

"Look at you, Sara! If I didn't see you, I never would've believed it."

"Was there a problem before?" she asked innocently.

"You know there was! You were scared breathless!"

Sara shrugged. "I think you're exaggerating!"

He laughed. Sara could tell that Jesse loved it when she teased him. It'd taken her a while to get comfortable enough to joke with him, about the time that they had first made love.

"Shall we get going?" Jesse asked. "Mount up."

This was probably her last time on horseback and that saddened her. If she wanted to ride again, she'd have to travel to a stable somewhere on the outskirts of Henderson Falls, and she couldn't get a very gentle horse that was personally screened by Jesse.

Sitting tall on Midnight, she looked over at Jesse.

He always seemed at one with Sunshine, totally comfortable and in control. She still flopped around on horseback, no matter how many times he instructed her to keep her legs and feet still.

Mickey was going to miss his horse, too. Socks had become a part of Mickey's heart, like a pet. Sara had thought about getting Mickey a dog, but she had never made the final decision. She was working, Mickey was in school, and when they weren't doing either of those things, they were going to counseling appointments. There wasn't any time to take care of a dog, and that would be unfair to the poor animal.

Maybe someday that would change. Someday.

"There's an easy trail that you haven't been on yet. I took the wranglers who are going to be in the trail ride rodeo there the other day."

"What's the trail ride rodeo?"

"Groups of riders will be on the trail at various intervals, and they will be judged by certain factors, like not bouncing in the saddle too much, and having a good time. Things like that. Mickey has a good chance of winning."

"There will be no living with him if he wins," Sara said.

"Socks is a great horse, and she loves Mickey. She'll do whatever Mickey wants."

They paused at the trailhead. "I'm going to miss our rides, Jesse. A lot."

"Me, too." Jesse pointed to the right path. "And I'm going to miss our talks."

Sara turned off to the right. "And our yoga and meditation."

"Yup."

"And I loved making love with you." Sara's face heated. She'd never said anything like that to a man before. Actually, there hadn't been the right man in her life to say it to, until Jesse.

Jesse turned to her and winked. "Today's Monday. The Camp Care Rodeo is on Saturday. We still have five days together."

"And it's going to be five days of craziness. The chuck wagon staff has to get ready for the big barbecue on Saturday. Parents, guardians and siblings are all invited and we are going to make mountains of food—salads, mac and cheese, ziti, meatballs, six types of cookies—you name it, and Cookie's serving it. And Cookie believes in everything being made from scratch, and that means made by us."

"If I can find a roving ramrod or five who isn't assigned to other duties for the rodeo, we'll just have to manage to meet in the evening."

"What are the roving ramrods doing for the rodeo?" Sara asked.

"Organizing artwork, ceramics, archery, swimming and whatnot. Looks like Camp Care goes all out. And I understand that every kid gets some kind of award at the ceremony on Saturday after dinner at the chuck wagon."

Sara sighed. "We'll be cleaning the kitchen after midnight and getting everything ready for the girls' program to start, and that includes making a bunch of bagged lunches. August is for the girls. They'll be moving in Sunday."

As the horses walked down the forest path, Sara and Jesse were quiet, each lost in their own thoughts.

Sara liked the sound of the horses' hooves on the packed dirt and how the leather squeaked, and seeing the way their heads bobbed up and down when they walked. The scents of cedar and pine wafted around her, and she appreciated the way the sunlight mottled the woods.

Henderson Falls had its own charm, but Camp Care's acreage was amazing. To see it on horseback was way different than what she was used to. To see it with Jesse was perfect.

"I'm going to miss this, Jesse. Won't you?" Sara shook her head. "Of course not. What a goofy question. You have your own ranch."

"Yup. I do."

"So you won't miss Camp Care."

"Sure I will. But it's really the people I'll miss, like my wranglers, but I told them if they ever got to Beaumont, Oklahoma, to look me up. I have lots of room in one of our bunkhouses, and that goes for you and Mickey. I mean it. Actually, the two of you can stay in the main house."

"That's nice of you."

"I'm not just being nice, Sara. I mean it."

Her heart did a little flip. "Thanks, Jesse. I might take you up on that if I can't get a job."

"Yeah. Come on down to Beaumont. I'm there when I'm not on the road, and if I'm not there nor my brothers, my sisters-in-law, Amber and Callie, should be home."

"They both sound like fun."

"They definitely are."

"Jesse, if I don't get a chance to be with you again, I'd like to thank you for a wonderful month. I'll never, ever forget you."

"I'll never forget you, Sara. You're a very special woman. And I'm sorry that I couldn't get Mickey to speak. He's so close. So damn close, and as long as we still have five days, I'm going to keep on trying."

"He definitely is real close to talking. I can feel it. He's showing emotion now and is participating in activities."

"I know he is, and giving Mickey *Black Beauty* to read was a stroke of genius."

Jesse laughed. "I also gave him last year's *PBR World Finals* book. He can't put that down, either."

"Thanks so much. I'll see to it that you get it back."

He shook his head from side to side. "Let him keep it. And later get him *My Friend Flicka*, *National Velvet*, and *Misty of Chincoteague*. All horse stories. He'll love them."

"You're a doll, Jesse Beaumont. Just a doll. And if we weren't on horseback, I'd give you a big fat kiss."

"Later!" He laughed. "But right now, we'd better start back, it's getting dark out. And I'll claim that kiss in the barn when we are brushing our horses, and more!"

"My pleasure!"

* * *

A couple days later, the whole camp turned out to watch the unloading of the Beaumont bulls.

The trucks rolled in a few hours after lunch.

The Beaumont brothers and their ranch hands placed thick steel fencing in a large square for a pen. More fencing was placed inside the square to make little cubicles for the bulls. Lastly, steel fencing was placed in two rows leading from the biggest truck.

A large door was released and fell into a type of ramp that led from the truck.

From her safe vantage point with the kitchen staff, Sara scanned the area for Mickey. He, too, was at a safe point, sitting on bleachers.

One by one, the bulls started to come down the ramp, down the fenced path and into the pen.

They were huge and ugly and smelly. Some had huge horns. Some had none. Some had big humps on their back. Some were minus the humps.

Where was Jesse? He was watching the bulls proudly with two other cowboys.

As soon as the animals were unloaded, Jesse started walking toward her with his brothers.

He waved to her to come over, and she walked toward the handsome trio. She knew they were Jesse's brothers. There was just something about how they stood with their thumbs through their belt loops, the way they smiled and how they tipped their hats.

"Sara, these are my brothers. That tall drink of water is Luke, and that handsome guy is Reed. Stay away from both. They're terrible teasers, so don't listen to a thing they say."

There were kisses and hand pumping from these two, with their dimples, sky blue eyes and cowboy hats. They were both handsome in jeans, long-sleeved shirts and boots with huge belt buckles and well-worn cowboy hats.

But Jesse was the handsomest man of the group.

Sara felt immediately comfortable with Luke and Reed. They teased like Jesse and were warm and outgoing.

"Some guys will do anything to get out of helping us build our houses," Reed said to Jesse.

"Yeah, some guys will even work at a kids' camp," joked Luke.

Jesse cleared his throat. "You know what, dear brothers? I love it here, and I'm thinking of expanding our equine therapy program at the ranch."

Reed shook his head. "That'd be a crazy undertaking, especially with all of us in the PBR."

"I won't be in the PBR forever," Jesse replied.

"From what Callie said, the hardest part of her job is the equine therapy program," Reed said. "Lots of paperwork. Lots of scheduling and a lot of people to work it."

"I could do it!" Sara said, then immediately bit her lip. She couldn't believe that she said that. "I mean, I could help with what I can from Henderson Falls."

"Naw, that won't work," Reed said. "It'd be better if you were there and working with Callie."

Luke looked at Sara, then at Jesse.

Jesse pulled Sara close to his side. "Let's think about the logistics, and see if a long-distance person could do the job. How's that? Reed can call his wife, Callie, and get her opinion. Callie does all the paperwork for the program now. In the meantime we'll sleep on it."

A job! And she'd be working from her house. It couldn't pay much, but she would find a way to make it work.

Since it was his idea, it definitely would be a way to keep in touch with Jesse. She'd work behind the scenes, and Jesse and his brothers would be the ramrods.

"Jesse, you said 'job.' Did you mean a paid job?"

"Of course!"

Working for Beaumont Ranch's equine therapy program would be ideal, both for her and for Mickey. She'd stay in touch with Jesse, and Mickey could continue to ride with Jesse's training.

Life has a funny way of working things out, doesn't it? she thought to herself.

Chapter 14

"Sara, since all of Camp Care is on the bleachers watching the bulls getting unloaded, I think that the Beaumont brothers should put on a little bull riding demonstration."

"Oh, Jesse! That would be a nice treat for everyone."

Especially me.

"I'll arrange it with Lori. She needs to keep everyone just where they are now—on the bleachers. No closer."

"I'd bet that a lot of these wranglers have never seen anyone ride a bull, like Mickey and me. They'll be ecstatic."

As she watched Jesse walk away, a thrill went through her body and settled in her stomach. Finally, she'd get the chance to see what a real bull rider did—what Jesse did—for a living.

Jesse spoke to Lori, gave a thumbs-up to his brothers, and then trotted back to the pens.

They were going to ride!

Mickey and the other wranglers of Bunkhouse 13 would be walking on air. Their ramrod could ride bulls. Certainly, that was a unique talent that he brought to his wranglers.

Oh! Sara hoped that Jesse would be careful. Damn. Another thing to worry about.

No. She was confident in Jesse's skills. The brothers wouldn't bring real tough bulls to a children's camp, would they?

She relaxed, unlike the rest of the wranglers, for whom the excitement was palpable, real. They couldn't sit still even if they were promised a week of free snacks from the canteen, but at least they stayed away from the bulls and on the bleachers.

A buzzer sounded and the spectators became silent. Everyone looked so serious until Luke came bursting out of the gate on a big black-and-white bull with horns. The cheering started, and didn't stop until another buzzer sounded and Luke jumped off. The bull trotted to an open gate and disappeared. Luke waved his arms and the cheering became louder.

When the buzzer went off again, Reed came out of the chutes on a white bull with black markings. It looked like Reed was going to fall off and there was a gasp from the crowd, but he righted himself and finished his ride. Everyone clapped and cheered.

Then it was Jesse's turn. Bunkhouse 13 screamed when Jesse came out of the chute. Those who could stand did so. She watched to see if Mickey would scream like the rest, but he didn't open his mouth. Not one sound. Jesse's black bull, with a big hump on his back, spun like a top. Then the bull reversed, Jesse stayed in control, and when the buzzer sounded Jesse let go of his rope and made a slick jump off that would do a gymnast proud.

Sara's emotions went haywire. She was thrilled, nervous and excited, all at the same time. And when he was finally safe, she felt relieved and limp.

When the bull had left the arena, Jesse bowed to the sound of Camp Care chanting his name: "Jesse! Jesse! Jesse!" She chanted the loudest.

The three Beaumont brothers all took a bow and announced that there would be a competition with more bull riders on Saturday morning. Some friends of theirs volunteered to be at Camp Care, too, and ride for the audience.

Sara wondered how Jesse could ride in the bull riding event because he was slated to run the wranglers' riding competition.

She shrugged and headed to the chuck wagon to finish cleaning up.

The first person she ran into was Cookie. "What a great show. Those Beaumont cowboys really can ride. They have guts. And those bulls…" He shook his head. "Amazing."

She smiled. "Yes. Absolutely amazing." And Jesse was the best. She hoped he'd win the Finals in Vegas. Though Mickey could watch all his events on TV, it wouldn't be the same.

As Sara scrubbed the big pots, unwanted tears pooled in her eyes. She would miss Jesse more than she expected. She hadn't even liked him at the beginning of Camp Care, but now...now...

She really liked him and couldn't imagine her life without him.

"Sara, you had a call in the office on the land line," Lori Floyd said. "Here's the number." Lori handed her a piece of paper. "Go ahead, the office is open. He said it was important."

She wondered who on earth it could be.

Oh! She recognized the number. Her old employer. Junior Ryan of Charles Ryan and Son Appliances.

"Junior, it's Sara Peterson. Did you call me?"

"I'll make this quick. I want you back. My wife can't get the swing of things, so I fired her, and I want you back. Start tomorrow?"

"You want me back? I don't know, Junior—the way you let me go was hurtful."

"I'll give you a ten percent raise and a company car."

"Gee, I don't know. I was offered another job and I'm definitely going to take it."

She could work remotely for Jesse and his equine therapy program and work for Junior; she'd just have to juggle her time.

"I don't know, Junior. How about twenty percent and a late model company car, not one of your junkers, and another three weeks' vacation?"

"Done. So you're coming back?"

"Yes. In a week."

"Whatever." He hung up.

Sara rinsed the pot and set it on the drain area of the sink. Then reached for another one.

So she had her old job back. What a relief!

Funny how life worked.

Junior was a nutcase, but she knew how to handle him. Besides, a twenty percent raise, a car and an extra three weeks of vacation was nothing to sneeze at. That settled that.

With the extra money, she wouldn't have to move. She and Mickey could even travel to a few of Jesse's PBR events!

But it wouldn't be the same as Camp Care. Here they spent every available minute together.

Traveling to visit him with Mickey...that wouldn't be the same, either. It would be better if she watched him on TV. Then maybe he wouldn't feel that she was stalking him, or that she couldn't let go.

"Hey, beautiful!"

"Jesse! Hey, you sure can ride bulls!" she replied.

"And you can sure scrub pots!"

"And this one is especially challenging—burnt-on mashed potatoes."

"I have some bad news for you."

Sara gripped his forearms with her soapy hands. "Oh, no! Is Mickey okay?"

"Mickey's fine," he said quickly. "But you can't help with the equine program at the ranch. Callie said that you need to be on-site to help her. And there's a lot of things to do when the kids are here."

"I understand." She nodded. What a disappointment. She would have liked to help out to keep in touch with Jesse, but she really did understand. "I have some good news."

"Hit me with it."

"I'm getting my old job back with a hefty raise, and other benefits."

"Oh. That is good news. Good for you." But Jesse didn't act like it was good news at all. His voice was monotone and his smile didn't look genuine.

"Let's celebrate!" he said. "Let's go to town and find someplace to talk. I'd like my brothers to get to know you."

"That's nice of you, Jesse, but I have at least another two hours here at the sink, the dishwasher and putting everything away after it's dry."

"Then I'll bring my brothers to you. We can help you with your kitchen duties, and we can talk in the main room over coffee."

"That's really nice, but they shouldn't have to do my work." It would be fun to get to know Jesse's brothers, but she should do her own work, and she'd better push Jesse away a bit, or she was going to be a mess when she got into her car to drive away.

"My mother taught us boys like we were studying for graduate degrees in the domestic arts. She didn't want our future wives to blame her if we couldn't cook, or sew, or do laundry, or clean, or wash dishes. I'm quite the catch."

He definitely was quite the catch. Some lucky woman would be happy to have him.

She sighed, feeling empty. That lucky woman wouldn't be her.

The Beaumont brothers scrubbed, dried, washed and put away pots and pans, dishes and silver. Reed and Luke even mopped the floor.

Cookie was tickled at having the top three bull riders in the world working hard in his kitchen.

"Go. Everyone. And thanks for your help," Cookie finally said. "There's a fresh pot of coffee ready and some cookies. Go, sit down. Enjoy."

After goodbyes to Cookie, they settled down at one of the long tables.

"Tell me about Amber and Callie," Sara said.

Luke grinned. "Amber is the sheriff of Beaumont County and is six months pregnant."

"And Callie runs the Beaumont Ranch and runs us. My wife is a tornado," Reed said proudly. "What about you, Sara?"

"I am the accountant and the office manager for a family-owned appliance store in Henderson Falls, New York. It's small potatoes, but I like my job."

"Callie is an accountant, too," Jesse said. "Sounds like you and she would work great together. I'm sorry that you need to be at the Beaumont Ranch to help her with our equine therapy program."

Sara smiled slightly, and Jesse could see that she would have liked to help. Darn it.

"Sounds like you and Callie would have a lot in common," Reed said.

"I think that I'd like both your wives," Sara said.

"Sara has a son, Mickey, who's in Camp Care. You'll see him when my classes do their riding demonstration Saturday morning. He's leading the first ride. He's quite the horseman."

"Sounds good," Luke said. "So, you can't ride bulls Saturday?"

"No. Count me out. It'll work out because you two definitely need the practice, and so do the other bull riders that you brought. I don't." Jesse winked at Sara, and she laughed.

When Sara laughed, it warmed his heart. It took her mind off her problems. The job problem was solved, but Mickey still hadn't talked. That was disappointing to Jesse. He'd promised Sara that the little wrangler would talk.

Who am I to make such a promise?

He still had three days left for Mickey. During the month, Jesse had come to feel like more than just a ramrod to Mickey. He felt like a father figure to the boy. Mickey was a great kid. He helped out his fellow campers; he had been one of the first to call attention to the electrical fire; he was a great reader and horseman, and was just an all-around likable kid.

His other nonspeaking wranglers had each managed to say a few words about their horses during one exercise that Jesse developed—and Jesse was walking on sunshine over that—but Mickey was still silent.

Luke, Reed and Sara were chatting up a storm. His brothers liked Sara, he could tell, and that was important to him. This was going to make his split from her even more painful.

They also wanted to meet the wranglers of Bunkhouse 13, particularly Mickey. They were going to drop by tomorrow morning.

As it turned out, Jesse's brothers couldn't make it the following morning because they were tending a bull with a sore hoof. The next day, however, they came to Bunkhouse 13. There the three of them told stories of the rank bulls—the bulls that scored the highest—that they rode, and the ones who got away.

Jesse's wranglers were thrilled beyond belief.

After they left, the Bunkhouse voted that they wear the bandannas that Jesse had given them when they rode their horses tomorrow.

Jesse thought that wearing the bandannas was like they were riding for the brand: Bunkhouse 13.

Jesse had decided that there wouldn't be any more riding today. The wranglers needed to say goodbye to one another and the horses needed to be washed and curried by Bunkhouses 3 and 6 and 10, who had drawn the short straws.

Jesse took a walk to the lake to his and Sara's spot. He did some stretches and sat crossed-legged, trying to clear his mind.

As if everyone hadn't had enough of Jesse and his

brothers, later, after dinner, they were going to discuss bull riding and conduct a question and answer session for the whole camp.

Camp Care was buzzing, and Jesse had heard that Cookie and his staff, and that meant Sara, were going to dish out ice cream, serve cookies and provide a vat of lemonade for everyone.

Nice.

He was happy that Sara had gotten along with his brothers. They'd raved about her this morning. That was great to hear.

And then there was his father, Big Dan Beaumont. Big Dan was once a big, booming man, but alcohol had him in its grip, and in turn, so did the Beaumont County Probation Department. They weren't going to let go until he was rehabilitated.

Big Dan was coming around thanks to rehab, his probation officer and his girlfriend's great cooking.

Jesse wanted Sara to meet Big Dan someday. He'd like her. His dad would take an immediate shine to Mickey, too.

Jesse took a deep breath, wondering why he'd been thinking about Sara meeting his family. He'd never thought about introducing anyone he'd been dating before.

Dating? Seemed such a casual word based on what he and Sara had shared this past month.

Only a month? It seemed like he'd known Sara forever.

So, tonight she was going to be busy, but so was

he. Tomorrow was going to be crazy, with the bull riding demo and the Camp Care Rodeo and cookout.

The wranglers would remember it forever. Heck, so would he. Plus, he doubted if he'd ever forget Sara.

He'd have to try.

"Jesse?" He heard her voice as she approached their meditation spot.

"Sara!"

"I only have a minute, but I wanted to say goodbye. I don't know when we'll have another chance to get together."

"You mean here? Or when we get home?" he asked.

"I meant here, but unfortunately it goes for home, too."

Jesse felt lonely already. In spite of all the women who regularly hung around him and whom he'd dated in the past, there weren't many whom he wanted to go out with again. He'd never seen a future with them like he did with Sara. Besides, none of them were like her.

Jesse managed a smile. "Yeah. We are lucky to both have jobs that we like."

"Oh, I know! I never thought I'd say this, but I've missed my job, and all the people there."

"You really miss it, huh?" Jesse asked. He hoped like hell that she'd suddenly changed her mind and that it was the worst job on the planet.

"I do, Jesse. And the extra money will be wonderful."

Jesse reached out and pulled her close. "I'm going to miss you like crazy."

Tears pooled in her eyes. "I'll miss you, too. This has been a fabulous month. I really needed someone like you, Jesse."

"And you've been just what I needed, too. Just who I wanted. Thanks for everything."

"And thanks for taking care of Mickey."

"I didn't get him to talk, although I keep thinking he's on the verge of a breakthrough."

"I do, too. I really do." Sara smiled. "And I'm not saying that lightly."

"Call me when it happens."

"You'll be the first. Then his teachers, psychologists, counselors, psychiatrists and whoever else has tried to help us."

She kissed him tenderly, then passionately. He could taste her salty tears when she broke contact.

"Don't cry, Sara. Think of the next time we can get together. We can plan, and then maybe, maybe—"

"Maybe we can get together when the PBR comes to Madison Square Garden in January. It's only six months away. Half of a year."

"Dammit. That sounds like a long time."

She smiled slightly. "It depends, I guess."

"On what?"

"On what I'm doing. If I'm busy or not," she said. "Speaking of which, I have to go now, Jesse. The kitchen is crazy, and so is Cookie. I've never seen him like this."

Jesse hugged her closer, tighter. "See you, Sara. I'll miss you."

"See you, Jesse. I'll miss you, too, but I'll see you in a while for your bull riding speech."

"I almost forgot."

"The wranglers haven't. They are flying. They had canteen today. I shudder to think how they'll be when Cookie sugars them up again later tonight."

He kissed Sara. He opened his eyes this time, wanting to remember every moment: the glint of her hair, their favorite spot and the way the sunbeams danced on the lake…

With a slight wave, Sara turned and walked in the direction of the chuck wagon.

And he missed her already.

Sara asked Cookie to let her be the one to finish cleaning up, since she'd scooted out to meet Jesse earlier. He saluted her, handed her the key and told her to get some rest for "tomorrow's nonstop chow-fest buffet that would go on all day long."

An hour earlier, the rain came without warning. No thunder or lightning, just a downpour of epic proportions.

At first she panicked, and started worrying about Mickey should the thunder and lightning hit. As she put the silverware away in the correct containers, she knew that Jesse would take excellent care of Mickey.

And just as soon as it came, the downpour went. Finally, she was done.

Then the rain hit again, and Sara wanted to hurry to her bunkhouse before she got too soaked.

She didn't see the top step of the stairs, and she fell, face-first, down the seven stairs. She remembered tasting mud and rainwater before she passed out.

"The rain is really coming down tonight," Jesse said to his bunkhouse wranglers. "I hope it stops so everyone can ride tomorrow. Hey, look out your windows and tell me if there's much water on the ground, will ya? My brothers will be mad and the wranglers will be sad if the rain keeps up. All that work…"

"Mom! Mom!" A raw, raspy voice came from Mickey.

"Mickey?" Jesse said, half in shock. "It's okay. Just rain."

Jesse tried to act calm, so he wouldn't startle Mickey. But the boy spoke! It must be more than important. "Mom! Help my mom, Jesse!"

Jesse ran to the window and looked out. Someone was definitely lying facedown in a huge puddle at the end of the chuck wagon stairs.

"Sara!"

Mickey nodded, and went running out of the bunkhouse.

"Mom! We're coming, Mom!"

"Mickey, wait!" He didn't want the boy to hurt himself catching a sneaker on a pothole or slipping on wet stones.

Aww…the hell with it. The boy needed to see his mother.

They reached Sara in record time, and Jesse didn't want to lift her in case she had broken bones or a spinal or neck injury, but she was about to drown in the puddle. He'd seen many horrible bull riding injuries and none of them had terrified him like seeing Sara lying in the water did now.

He gently moved Sara onto her side.

"Sara, wake up. I have Mickey with me. We're worried about you." Jesse pushed back the hair from the side of her face and tucked it behind her ears. He held her head in his hand. "Talk to her, Mickey. Talk to your mom."

"Mom. This is Mickey Peterson. My real name is Michael James Peterson. Are you okay, Mom? Can you open your eyes? Your hair is really muddy. Your face is muddy, too. Are you going to be okay, Mom?"

Jesse realized that Mickey actually had been speaking full sentences!

What a thrill! Mickey had done it! But Jesse couldn't relish in his victory; he was too worried about Sara.

Chapter 15

Sara slowly came out of her thick, wet fog to the sound of Mickey talking. Mickey! This was what she'd waited two years for: the sound of her precious son's voice.

"Sara?"

That was Jesse's voice.

"I'm okay, Jesse."

"Don't move, Sara. The doctor is coming."

That was Jesse's voice, the cowboy that she loved. Yes, she loved him, but he'd never said that he loved her.

"I love you, Mom. Mom, wake up. I brought the doctor."

They moved her to a stretcher, carried her into the chuck wagon and gently laid her on a table.

"I'm Doctor Festerly. Do you know your name?"

"Yes." Everyone laughed.

"Do you mind telling me what it is?" the doctor asked.

"Sara Peterson."

"Do you think you can sit up?"

With help, she slowly sat up. Gently, Dr. Festerly took the wadded-up wet lump that was under her head. Sara realized it must be Jesse's shirt.

"Sara, do you know where you are?" the doctor asked.

"I was in a mud puddle. Now I'm in the chuck wagon."

The doctor laughed and held some gauze under her chin. "What hurts?"

"Every bone in my body, but mostly my chin."

She took a deep breath. "Where's Jesse?"

"I'm right here, Sara."

She took some clean gauze from the doctor and held it on her chin. "Thanks for being with me, Jesse. Did you hear Mickey talk?"

"I sure did, and, of course, I'd be with you."

She looked at the worried group. "Mickey, talk to me." She reached for the boy's hand and held it. "Give us a minute, Dr. Festerly. This is a big moment. So, tell me, what happened, son?"

"I was scared, Mom. I saw you fall down the stairs when I was looking out the window. I ran out of the bunkhouse. I was worried that when I called for help no one would come, like with Dad. When Dad got hurt, I yelled and yelled and no one came to help. And he died. And I stopped yelling. I stopped talking."

"Because no one came?" Sara asked.

Mickey nodded. "But Jesse came this time. He came and I ran for the doctor like he told me. And you're not going to die."

"Not yet, Mickey. I have a lot of living to do yet, and so do you. You're a cowboy now." She smiled. "Jesse?" Sara turned her head to look at him. "I'm okay."

He took her other hand. "Your chin is bleeding."

Sara rubbed her thumb on the back of Jesse's hand. "If that's the worst thing that happened out of that swan dive, I'll be fine."

"Tell me something else, Mickey. Tell me about Socks, your horse," Sara said.

Mickey told her that he was going to miss Socks, told her about each of his friends in Bunkhouse 13 and how much he really liked Jesse.

"And you like Jesse, too, don'tcha, Mom?"

"Yes. Sure. I like Jesse. He's been a good friend to me here," Sara said.

"And Jesse likes you. The whole camp knows that," said Mickey.

Jesse grinned. "The whole camp?"

"Uh-huh."

Her face heated, and not from her pain.

Later, Dr. Festerly examined Sara totally, telling her that she was fine, except for her chin, which needed three stitches, and the fact that she needed a shower to get the stones, mud and grit off her. She might see scrapes and bruises and some red marks, but they would all eventually go away.

That was great news. She didn't have to go to town for X-rays.

Soon the stitches were in along with adhesive tape, and she was headed to her bunkhouse to get a change of clothes, take a shower and take a couple of her over-the-counter pain meds.

She had a headache and was a little unsteady on her feet, but with Jesse on one side and Mickey on the other, she'd never been happier. It seemed like they were a little family, all walking together. She grinned. It was a nice feeling, probably for Mickey, too.

Jesse deposited Mickey at Bunkhouse 13, and checked on his wranglers. Roving Ramrod Ronnie was present.

"Thanks, Ronnie." Jesse held out his hand and they shook. "But hang on for a couple more minutes, okay? I have to say goodbye to Sara again."

Jesse jogged to Sara's shower and waited for her to reappear. When she saw him standing there, she jumped.

"I didn't mean to scare you, Sara. I just thought I'd check on you, but, hey, would you like me to wash your back?"

She shook her head. "Mr. Jesse Beaumont, what are you doing here at the door of the women's shower?"

"Hoping to catch you naked."

Sara rolled her eyes. "Are you in seventh grade or what?"

"Sixth."

"I'm feeling like a mess. I still have small stones everywhere, and my hair is gritty."

"I hear that some people pay thousands of dollars for that kind of treatment at a spa."

She chuckled. "Come here, bull rider."

When he did, she just let him hold her. "You did it, Jesse. You did it. Mickey spoke. He talked. He wouldn't shut up!" She cried into his dry blue shirt that matched his eyes.

"It wasn't me. It was just the circumstances of what happened. Mickey flashed back to the accident and gave it one more try, for you this time."

"But you let Mickey go to me. He told me that. If you made him stay in the bunkhouse—"

"I wouldn't have ever told him to stay inside. He needed to see if you were all right."

She dried her tears, and she pulled at a lock of her hair. "I need to shower. Then I need to get some sleep. I'm exhausted."

"I'll stay here until you come out. I want to make sure you're okay."

"That's not necessary, Jesse. I'll be fine."

"I'll wait. Then I'll walk you to your bunkhouse." He opened the door for her, and she walked in. "Yell if you need me to wash your back or something."

She laughed. Jesse always made her laugh.

Sara took a long hot shower, and washed her hair three times. She kept thinking about how nice it was that Jesse was waiting for her to see if she'd be all right.

She didn't want to say goodbye to him again, so when she was done, she wanted to go to bed.

"Thanks for watching out for me, Jesse," she said. "See you tomorrow, then?"

"We'll find some time to get together."

Jesse gave her a kiss good-night, and Sara didn't want him to stop.

She pulled away, though, gave him a kiss on the cheek, and walked away, before she decided to stay with Jesse all night.

Lori had changed the rodeo schedule so that everyone could watch the bull riding, and all of Camp Care filed into the bleachers after breakfast.

Cookie said that after the bull riding, the staff had to zoom into the kitchen to prepare for lunch.

Sara couldn't believe that today was the last day of Mickey's Camp Care.

She almost couldn't wait to get Mickey home so the two of them would be able to talk nonstop. But then she'd miss Jesse.

They all recited the Pledge of Allegiance, and then Jesse came out. "Welcome wranglers and ramrods and other staff. Welcome parents, guardians and caregivers. Welcome to the first event of the Camp Care Rodeo." There was a round of applause. "Our first bull rider is from Canada, Justin Fletcher. Let's see if he can ride for eight seconds."

Justin rode for six seconds before he got bucked off.

Four other riders all got bucked off. Then it was time for the Beaumont Brothers.

Reed and Luke rode, but Luke got bucked off.

They all rode again with varying results, but the three Beaumont brothers still showed that they were world champions.

"A big thanks to the Beaumonts for bringing their bulls to Camp Care. Now, stay put for the wranglers' horse riding, ladies and gentlemen," Lori said. "All entry riders, please go to the barn and saddle up!"

Sara wanted to see Mickey lead his group, and Jesse told her just where to sit, on the edge of the bleachers on the side by her bunkhouse.

Her heart was thumping and it was excruciating to wait. Finally, a bell rang, and Mickey walked Socks into the arena.

Jesse walked alongside Mickey, but didn't lead the horse. Mickey rode alone.

The riders executed a turn in the arena, and then stopped. Sara's heart soared. At the start of camp, she'd never believed in a million years that Mickey could ride a horse.

"The trophy for the most improved rider goes to Mickey Peterson," Jesse said into the microphone.

Lori Floyd handed Mickey a trophy. "Would you like to say something, Mickey?"

"Yes. I want to thank Socks, my mom and my ramrod, Jesse. Camp Care is really awesome."

Immediately, Sara began to cry. Loud, obnoxious tears. She pulled out some paper towels from her jeans that she grabbed from the kitchen because she knew she would cry and covered her mouth with them.

"My mom's crying." She heard Mickey say to Jesse. "It's my fault that she cries."

"Well, cowboy, sometimes moms cry when they're happy, and this is one of those time," Jesse replied. "She's happy that you're talking and are riding Socks."

"I love Socks, Jesse. I'm going to miss him."

"Mickey, I didn't tell you this before, but Socks is my horse. He comes from the Beaumont Ranch, and he's going back there when I go home. I'll take real good care of him, and I'll send you pictures. How's that?"

"Really?"

"Really."

That started a new batch of crying for Sara. Jesse was such a great guy.

The final goodbye to his bunkhouse pals was going to be really tough for Mickey. Saying goodbye to Socks was going to be like moving away from his best buddy.

Which was just what he was doing.

This was it. Sara and Mickey were packed and ready to go. From what Mickey told her, there had been a massive huddle in Bunkhouse 13 where they all sang Roy Rogers's "Happy Trails," led by Jesse. After the song ended, there was no sadness—just a lot of cheering and clapping. Mickey said Jesse shook every wrangler's hand as they left Bunkhouse 13 to meet their rides back home.

Mickey and Jesse stopped at Sara's bunkhouse to pick her up. Then all three of them went to the barn.

"I'm going to miss you, Socks," said Mickey, kissing the horse's great face. His tone was shaky and watery, but he held it together. "Jesse is going to send me your picture, Socks, and I'm going to put it in my room along with our trophy." Mickey spun around, quickly. "Let's go, Mom."

Jesse walked them to Sara's car. Mickey got in the back seat with a book. "I'll wait in here in case you guys want to talk."

"Thanks, cowboy," Jesse said. "But can I give you a handshake first?"

Mickey shook Jesse's hand, then it turned into a big hug. Jesse hugged him back. Tears stung Sara's eyes, but she blinked them back. She didn't want to do any more crying.

The car door closed as Mickey slid back in.

"Sara?"

"Yes, Jesse?"

"I'll call you and figure out how and when we can see each other. Is that okay with you?"

"Oh, yes!"

"And maybe someday you and Mickey can visit the Beaumont Ranch," he said. "And Mickey can visit Socks. Do you think you'd be interested in that?"

"Jesse, I was hoping you'd ask! And maybe you'd come visit us in Henderson Falls."

"New York? Uh…sure. Yes. I'll come visit."

"Jesse, I live in the suburbs in an apartment building. There's green space all around it and on the side there's a little park. I'm sure it's almost like your ranch!"

They both laughed, and Sara felt better.

"Then I guess that this is goodbye for now," he said.

Jesse, please tell me that you love me. I love you, I really do, she thought.

But Jesse remained silent, looking up at the sky, looking around the grounds. It seemed that he wanted to get rid of her because he ran out of things to say.

Her heart felt heavy in her chest. "I'll see you soon, then," Sara said keeping her head down, ready for those tears to fall. She walked to the driver's side of her car, quickly shut the door and hurriedly wiped her eyes. Then she rolled down the window.

"Do I get a kiss?" Jesse asked, with his head in the window.

Sara could barely talk, but she put her arms around his neck and gave him a quick peck on the lips. "I'd better get going, Jesse. Our plane leaves at two o'clock."

He stepped back from the car. "Yeah. Sure. Bye."

That was it? Sara backed up the car then drove down the gravel road that led to the main road. She kept looking at Jesse in her rearview mirror until he walked away.

Sara quickly settled into her routine at home. She and Mickey decided together which counseling appointments they should keep and which ones they could terminate.

School started after Labor Day, so Mickey still had a lot of vacation left, but all he did was draw pictures of Socks, talk about horses and look at Sara's phone, which contained pictures of his time at camp.

Then he nagged Sara into printing off the pictures from her cell phone, which she did, on glossy print paper that they bought at the store.

Jesse had called her once. He had asked Callie to set him up with some kind of program where they could see each other's "video," but Callie hadn't had the time yet because they were hosting an equine therapy program in two weeks.

Since the conversation between them seemed stilted and unnatural, Sara wasn't looking forward to any more calls. It wasn't the same as seeing him in person.

Maybe he was trying to give her a hint that he was moving on.

So, she moved on, too. She threw herself into her work at Charles Ryan and Son Appliances. She was happy to be back, but she'd rather be dishing out meals and scrubbing the chuck wagon's pots and pans.

It was the evenings, when she was lying in bed and trying to get to sleep that she thought about Jesse—how he looked, how he smiled, how they made love, how they did yoga together, they laughed, they rode horses and they had their own "spot."

"Mom! Hey, Mom! Come outside! It's totally awesome!"

Mickey probably wanted to show her another sports car in the parking lot outside that he wanted her to ask Junior for. He was convinced that the car from Junior was too old-looking.

"Mickey, I don't want to see any more sports cars. I'm folding laundry."

Mickey laughed. "It's not a car, believe me!" And then he was gone. She could hear Mickey shouting, and someone was shouting back.

She sighed. "I'm coming. I'm coming," she said to no one there.

And then she saw a familiar equine shape. The horse was munching on the patch of grass next to her building. Mickey was sitting on top of Socks, grinning from ear to ear.

Puzzled, she looked around. There was a truck with a horse trailer in the parking lot, with the Beaumont Ranch logo emblazoned on the side.

Jesse! He was dressed in his usual cowboy attire and holding a huge bouquet.

She held her breath, and she walked toward him.

Jesse took a knee. "I can't live without you, Sara. I think of you constantly, and I feel like half a man. Will you marry me and move to Beaumont? My brothers and I will build us a house. You can work for the ranch with Callie, if you'd like. I need you. I love you. I couldn't stand it when you drove away from me."

"Wait a minute!" Mickey said.

"Oh, Mickey! I apologize. As the man in the family, I should have asked your permission," Jesse said, getting up.

"If you marry my mom, do I get Socks?" Mickey asked.

Jesse laughed. "Is this a package deal?"

"You know it." Mickey kissed the horse's face, then ran to Jesse and hugged him.

"Sara, don't cry," said Jesse.

Mickey snorted. "It's a happy cry. My mom does that all the time. Tell Ramrod Jesse that you'll marry him, Mom."

"I thought you'd never ask! Of course I'll marry you, Ramrod Jesse!" She sniffed as Jesse handed her the flowers. "I love you, too."

Epilogue

The historic Beaumont Ranch was the setting of the marriage of Jesse Daniel Beaumont and Sara Jean Peterson of Henderson Falls, New York, on Saturday, October 2.

The bride's father, John Matty, gave the bride away.

Mr. Michael "Mickey" James Peterson served as the best man for the groom.

Bridesmaids were Mrs. Amber Beaumont and Mrs. Callie Beaumont. Matron of Honor was Mrs. Donna Weaver of Henderson Falls, New York.

Groomsmen were the groom's brothers, Mr. Luke Beaumont and Mr. Reed Beaumont.

During the reception held in the beautiful gardens on the premises, wedding attendees were treated to the unexpected, early birth of the first child of Amber and Luke Beaumont, a girl, Olivia Rose Beaumont, born in her father's bedroom in the Beaumont homestead.

The bride is employed by Beaumont Ranch as an administrative assistant and accountant.

In November, Mr. and Mrs. Jesse Beaumont will honeymoon in Las Vegas, Nevada, where the groom and his brothers will ride bulls at the Professional Bull Riders World Finals.

* * * * *

"The two of you are still married," Liz said.

"Still?" Lulu croaked.

Sam asked, "What are you talking about?"

"More to the point, how do you know this?" Lulu
demanded, the news continuing to hit her like a gut punch.

Travis looked down at the papers in front of him.
"Official state records show you eloped in the Double
Knot Wedding Chapel in Memphis, Tennessee, on
Monday, March 14, nearly ten years ago. Alongside
another couple, Peter and Theresa Thompson, in a double
wedding ceremony."

Lulu gulped. "But our union was never legal," she
pointed out, trying to stay calm, while Sam sat beside her
in stoic silence.

Liz countered, "Ah, actually, it is legal. In fact, it's still
valid to this day."

Sam reached over and took her hand in his, much as he had the first time they had been in this room together. "How is that possible?" Lulu asked weakly.

"We never mailed in the certificate of marriage, along with the license, to the state of Tennessee," Sam said.

"And for our union to be recorded and therefore legal, we had to have done that," Lulu reiterated.

"Well, apparently, the owners of the Double Knot Wedding Chapel did, and your marriage was recorded. And is still valid to this day, near as we can tell. Unless you two got a divorce or an annulment somewhere else? Say another country?" Travis prodded.

"Why would we do that? We didn't know we were married," Sam returned.

Don't miss
Their Inherited Triplets *by Cathy Gillen Thacker,*
available August 2019 wherever
Harlequin® Special Edition books and ebooks are sold.

www.Harlequin.com

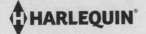

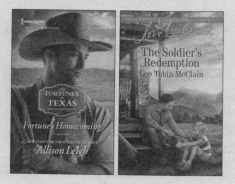

Love Inspired®

Inspirational Romance to Warm Your Heart and Soul

Join our social communities to connect with other readers who share your love!

Sign up for the Love Inspired newsletter at **www.LoveInspired.com** to be the first to find out about upcoming titles, special promotions and exclusive content.

CONNECT WITH US AT:

Facebook.com/groups/HarlequinConnection

 Facebook.com/LoveInspiredBooks

 Twitter.com/LoveInspiredBks

LISOCIAL2018

Love Harlequin romance?

DISCOVER.

Be the first to find out about promotions, news and exclusive content!

 Facebook.com/HarlequinBooks

Twitter.com/HarlequinBooks

 Instagram.com/HarlequinBooks

Pinterest.com/HarlequinBooks

ReaderService.com

EXPLORE.

Sign up for the Harlequin e-newsletter and download a free book from any series at **TryHarlequin.com.**

CONNECT.

Join our Harlequin community to share your thoughts and connect with other romance readers!
Facebook.com/groups/HarlequinConnection

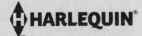 **HARLEQUIN®**

**ROMANCE WHEN
YOU NEED IT**